RETRIBUTION

Richard Hawke

This book is devoted to the love of my life, Pauline

Sam Clark was thoroughly pissed off. Soaked to the skin from the unrelenting rain, cold and hungry, he had absolutely no reason to be otherwise. He'd just spent most of the morning on the streets scavenging for food and ended up with precious little for his efforts. A couple of apples pinched from a greengrocer was going to have to do for both his breakfast and lunch today. He'd have to go out again later to get something for his dinner; hopefully the rain would have stopped by then. Unless, of course, his mother came back with some food. He wasn't holding his breath on that though!

Pausing at the entrance to the sixth floor flat, he took a deep breath, knowing what he was going to find inside. Pushing the door open, his nostrils were immediately as-sailed by an appalling stench comprised of body odour, excreta, vomit and God only knew what else.

Grimacing, he went in. His father was still slumped on the filthy, worn out sofa. Totally out of his head from the cocktail of drugs and alcohol that he had taken just

minutes after emerging from his previous drug and alcohol induced stupor, he lay on his front, his head lolling
over the edge of the seat. A drool of vomit and spittle
hung from his slack lips. Empty vodka bottles used syringes and other drug paraphernalia littered the stained,
thread-bare carpet beneath him.

Clad in nothing but dirty socks and soiled underpants,
John Clark was about as sorry and pathetic a human being as it was possible to be. From school, he'd gone
straight into a life of petty crime, drugs and alcohol. Like
most of his type, he had been cute enough though to take
advantage of everything the social services had to offer –
unemployment benefit, medical care and free housing.
The latter was, indeed, the only reason he had married
Sam's mother and then immediately fathered the boy. A
wife and child vastly increased the chances of getting a
council home, even it was just a dingy flat.

Twenty-eight years old, Clark had never done a day's
work in his life. Indeed, he had abused his brain and body
to such a degree, he was quite incapable of work, or anything else for that matter. The drugs had such a grip on
him that he was now almost totally helpless. He never left
the flat, which was just as well as it was extremely unlikely
he could have safely negotiated the six flights of stairs.
Being a council building, the lift, needless to say, was almost always out of order.

Barely able to walk, he spent virtually his entire life now
on the reeking sofa. About the only time he left it was to
stumble to the bathroom or kitchen. What little he ate
was usually eaten there, he slept there, and he even went

to the toilet there when he couldn't make it to the bathroom.

Normally, Sam gave his father a very wide berth and
basically ignored him as much as possible. He had no real
feelings for the man; why should he? His father had never
done a thing for him; he felt no love, no hate, no sympathy – there was just nothing there.

He was about to go into his room when he suddenly
became aware of the unnaturally loud and laboured
breathing coming from the sofa. Glancing across at his
father, he could see the man was in an even worse state
than usual. Not only was his breathing bad, he was muttering incoherently, sweating profusely and on the point
of falling off the sofa to the floor.

Walking over, he stared down and, for a second or two,
considered helping him. He could at least pull him back
onto the sofa if nothing else. On the verge of doing it, a
sudden feeling of disgust and utter contempt washed
over him. At just ten years of age, he was having to scav-
enge the streets to feed and clothe himself while this pathetic wreck of a human being spent a large part of the
already meagre household income on drugs and booze
for himself.

Spinning on his heel, he walked away. Going into his
room, he pulled an apple from his pocket, threw himself
down on the bed and started eating it hungrily. As he ate,
it occurred to him that his father could drop dead at any
time and he really wouldn't give a shit.

A couple of hours or so later, Sam was playing a game
on his iPad when the banging of the front door heralded

the arrival of his mother. Rebecca Clark was 27, just a year younger than her husband, and basically headed in the same direction. While she wasn't yet into hard drugs like the heroin and cocaine he took, she was an increasingly frequent user of cannabis and swallowed sleeping pills like they were going out of fashion. She was also a heavy drinker and drank at least two bottles of cheap red wine most days. To fund it all, plus what little she put into the household budget, she had turned to prostitution.

Sam had scarcely any more time for her than he did his father. She was a cold, detached woman who appeared to have no feelings for her only child at all. Indeed, the only emotion he got from her was obvious irritation at having to house him. He could, however, at least have some semblance of a conversation with her at times – something that was impossible with his wreck of a father.

Getting up, he went out and found her in the kitchen stacking wine bottles in the rusting old fridge.

Standing in the doorway, he watched as she placed the last bottle in the fridge. Although she hadn't looked round, he knew she was aware of him. Straightening and still not looking at him, she opened a pack of cigarettes, put one in her mouth and lit it. Moving over to the window, she stood staring out while she smoked, all the while ignoring him.

She had been an attractive woman but the stress of living with a drug addict, plus her own lifestyle, was catching up with her. Painfully thin, her face was flushed, her eyes puffy and bloodshot. When she spoke, her voice was raspy from the chain smoking.

'Did you bring anything to eat?' She probably hadn't but it was something with which to break the awkward silence.

'No,' she muttered dully.

Already he could see he was wasting his time; today was one of those days when she just didn't want to know.

He tried again. 'He's not too good today,' nodding in the direction of the living room. 'You should take a look at him.'

'Fuck him and fuck you,' she snapped. 'I don't give a shit. Just leave me alone.' Still not looking at him, she stalked over to her bedroom and disappeared inside slamming the door behind her.

Sam shook his head dispiritedly. 'What a pair,' he thought to himself. He knew she would sleep now and then reappear in the early evening when she would start on the wine. At about 10.00 she would get dolled up and then disappear out. Even at his young age, he knew and understood what she was getting up to; he'd had a hard introduction to life and was aware of things years before he should have been.

Shrugging, he glanced at his watch, the one he'd stolen from a stall at Surrey Street Market a few months ago. It said 2.30pm – another couple of hours and it would be dark. It was time he ventured out again and got something to eat for his dinner. He didn't give his father even a cursory glance as he left. Heading down the stairwell that led to the street below, he was blissfully unaware that his already miserable life was about to become even more miserable.

The flat was in a tower block called Cromwell House, located at the top end of East Street in the Broad Green district of Croydon. It was one of the distinctly less salubrious parts of the world in which to live, the area having high crime and unemployment rates. The streets in Broad Green were uniformly shabby and uninspiring, and East Street was one of the worst.

Sam was meeting his friend Paul, who lived a few streets away. Unlike Sam, he had good parents who looked after him well and he certainly had no need to go thieving. Being a good-natured lad and aware of his friend's unfortunate circumstances, he did his best to help him out as much as he could. Plus, for some reason Sam could never understand, he seemed to get a considerable buzz from thieving and the inherent risk of being caught.

The boys had agreed to meet at the Cafe Nero coffee shop, which was about twenty minutes walk away. Mooching along disconsolately, Sam couldn't help but feel despondent. The nasty outburst from his mother had affected him more than it usually did. As a rule, he didn't take too much notice of her unpleasantness but today it had got to him. Although he didn't realise it, the dreadful condition his father was in was having a depressing effect on him as well.

Approaching the coffee shop, he could see his pal, hands in pockets, slouching in his usual casual fashion. Normally, the sight would have cheered him up but not today.

From his listless approach, it was immediately apparent to Paul that Sam was in one of his brooding moods. It wasn't uncommon and while he understood why, it didn't alter the fact that his friend could be a right pain-in-the-ass when he was like this.

'Things not so good?' he asked sympathetically.

Sam sighed and shook his head. 'Never seen him so bad. I wouldn't be surprised if he's pegged it by the time I get back.' He kicked an empty beer can irritably into the road earning himself an angry glare from a passing cyclist.

There was an awkward pause before Paul, not knowing quite how to respond, said rather lamely, 'What do you want to do then?'

Sam shrugged. There was actually very little provision in the Broad Green area for bored kids. Facilities like parks, leisure centres, youth clubs, etc were non-existent. About the only place of any interest was Carey's Amusement Arcade over in Penywern Road where the boys could while away an hour or two playing video games. When they had some money that was!

'You got any cash on you?'

Paul shook his head. That was the amusement arcade blown out!

'I could do with something to eat; all I've had today is a couple of apples.'

'Come on then, let's just walk and see what turns up.'

It wasn't long before they happened upon a butcher's shop. Rather grandiosely titled "Gilbert's Fresh Meat Emporium", it was a shabby, dirty looking place that knowledgeable locals gave a wide berth. Peering in through the grimy plate glass window, they could see the shop was empty apart from the butcher himself who was busily engaged in cutting up a carcass. Paul glanced questioningly at Sam, 'What do you reckon?'

'Yeah, this'll do.'

Taking a look around to make sure they weren't being watched, Paul nodded at Sam. 'Okay, let's do it.' He waited while Sam crossed the street and hid behind a bus shelter opposite. Then he ran into the shop yelling loudly, 'An old lady has just collapsed outside. She looks in a bad way. Can you help please?'

He had done it many times before and was very convincing. Concern on his face, the butcher came hurrying out from behind the counter, wiping his hands on his greasy apron.

Hopping from foot to foot in apparent urgency and impatience, Paul yelled, 'Come on, she's just around the corner over there.' He pointed at a side street about twenty metres away. With the man behind him, he took off at speed. The butcher struggled to keep up and quickly fell behind.

Sam, meanwhile, had nipped across the road into the now empty shop. After a quick look around, he slipped two large pork pies, a ham and some sausage rolls into a carrier bag. No more than sixty seconds later, he strolled casually out into the sunshine.

Out in the street, Paul had no intention of stopping – he simply kept on running. The butcher would stop after twenty or thirty metres; they always did.

Having done it numerous times before without any

problems, the thought that this time he might get caught never entered Sam's head. It came as a distinct shock, therefore, when he suddenly felt a firm hand on his shoulder. Looking up, he saw a tall man in his thirties, casually dressed in jeans and bomber jacket, eyeing him suspiciously. 'What are you up to?'

Sam had had enough of adults for one day. 'Fuck off,' he said belligerently. Vainly, he twisted and turned in an attempt to wriggle free but the man had too tight a grip.

'I asked you a question lad. What were you doing in the butcher's shop?' His voice was sharp.

'It's none of your fucking business. Now piss off and leave me alone.'

'What a charming little boy,' he said sarcastically. 'Well, I'm sorry but it is my business. I'm a policeman and I'm pretty sure you've been shoplifting.' He pointed at the carrier bag. 'What have you got there?'

The copper had him bang-to-rights and Sam knew it. With a muttered curse, he handed the bag over.

At that moment, the butcher came panting up to them. His face was angry as he exclaimed, 'Bloody kids mucking around. I could have been robbed thanks to that little sod.' He turned to the policeman. 'Your lot need to get a grip Mr Davis.'

'Hello Gilbert. Actually, I think you *have* been robbed.' Holding the bag out, he asked, 'Is this stuff yours?'

The butcher took a quick peek. 'Yes.' Looking at Sam, he said furiously, 'And I assume this little bastard stole it.'

Davis nodded. 'Unfortunately for him, I saw the whole

thing. I was just coming up the street on my way here to get some bones for the dog when I saw you and a boy come running out. Then this one went in and a minute or so later came back out with this bag.'

'Honestly Mr Davis, it's getting really bad around here. The bloody immigrants are the worst – they come in and ....'

'We're aware of the issues Gilbert.' Davis cut him short swiftly. 'Let's stick to the matter at hand. What about the lad? Do you want to take this further?'

The butcher face screwed his face up angrily then sighed and shook his head. 'No, I suppose not. I've got the stuff back so there's no point really.' He glared at Sam, 'But if I ever see you again.'

The policeman nodded. 'Okay. Now then, about the bones for the dog?'

'I'll get them. While you're here can I tempt you with a nice piece of fresh fillet steak?' Gilbert enquired hopefully.

'No thanks,' Davis said wryly. He'd sampled Gilbert's meat once before and wasn't about to do it again. The bones were all right though. Percy, his Labrador, wasn't fussy.

When they were back outside, he put his hand on the boy's shoulder. 'I'll take you home and have a word with your parents.'

'Good luck with that,' Sam snorted derisively.

The policeman gave him a curious glance; the boy had a strangely adult way of speaking and he was beginning to get the feeling there was maybe more to him than he'd initially thought.

When they were seated in his car, Davis turned to him. 'What's your name?'

'Sam Clark.'

'And where do you live Sam?'

'608 Cromwell House, East Street, Croydon.' Now the initial shock of being apprehended had worn off, he was resigned to what was happening.

Davis grimaced. He was well acquainted with the flats at Cromwell House. Dingy and dirty, they were infested with the dregs of humanity – drug addicts, dealers, alcoholics, whores and other assorted low-life's.

It wasn't just Cromwell House either; the surrounding area was much the same, and he and his colleagues spent a disproportionate amount of their time there. With an inkling now of what he was going to find, he began to feel a bit more sympathetic towards the boy.

A few minutes later they pulled up outside the building. Looking up at the grey, grimly depressing tower block, the policeman was reminded, as he always was when he came to this awful place, of the day they had raided one of the top floor flats. Acting on a tip-off, they had burst in on a "paedophile party" and what they had found made even the hardest of them sick to their stomachs. Davis had only just joined the police at the time and was already wondering if it was going to be the right career for him. What he saw that day had convinced him it was.

Wondering what he was going to find this time, he escorted the boy up the filthy, litter-strewn, stairwell to the sixth floor. Stopping at number 608, Sam muttered, 'Are you sure you want go in here?'

Once again, Davis was struck by the boy's adult manner. The policeman was beginning to suspect he was one of life's unfortunates – he knew the signs all too well.

'Come on, open it.'

'Don't say I didn't warn you.' Unlocking the door, Sam stood aside to let the policeman enter. The first thing that struck Davis was the smell; he'd been in some pretty foul places before and this was the equal of any of them. The room was pitch dark with the lights off and curtains drawn.

'Can we have some light in here? I can't see a thing,' he asked, almost afraid at what might be revealed. The boy flicked a switch on the wall and a naked bulb dimly flickered into life. Moving over to the window, he pulled the curtains open, letting in more light.

'Could you open the window as well please?' The stench was dreadful.

'Sorry, it's jammed shut. Doesn't work – like just about everything in this shithole,' Sam's voice was matter-of-fact.

Davis wasn't surprised. Standing just inside the door, he looked around the shabby room with disgust. Below his feet, the ragged carpet was stained with God only knew what, wallpaper was peeling away from the walls, and there were patches of mouldy damp on the ceiling. Everything was covered in a thick layer of dust and the room clearly hadn't been cleaned in a long, long time. Alongside the far wall was a ragged sofa with a man lying on it.

Moving over for a closer look, Davis could see he was in a wretched condition. On his back, head lolling to one side, the sorry creature was naked apart from filthy underpants and had clearly messed himself. Adding to the stench was a considerable amount of vomit, both on him and the floor below. After a few moments, Davis was pretty sure he was looking at a corpse. The man's mouth was slack, his eyes were vacant and he didn't appear to be breathing. Reaching down, the policeman gave the body a nudge but there was no response. Picking up a limp arm, he felt at the inside of the wrist for a pulse but there wasn't one. As he did so, he noticed the veins were blue and had collapsed. The hand was also extremely cold. All the indications were that he had been a drug addict and had overdosed.

Laying the arm down gently, he examined the paraphernalia on the floor next to the sofa. Amongst plates of rotting food, empty bottles, cigarette packets and other assorted debris, he noticed a bag containing a white powder. Next to this were a couple of tablespoons, a bottle of citric acid, a bottle of water, a lighter and some syringes. Together, they comprised the typical heroin addict's tool kit and confirmed his diagnosis of drug overdose. Commonly, heroin is placed into a spoon, mixed with water and citric acid, and then heated in the spoon using a lighter or candle until it becomes liquefied. Then it is injected into a vein.

Looking at the man's body again, he saw how emaciated it was. Together with the hollow eyes and sunken cheeks, it made him look much older than he actually was. The face and arms were covered in numerous scabs where he had been picking at himself. The latter was a side effect of opiate withdrawal that triggers the urge to pick or rub at the skin. Both were indications of heroin addiction.

Sights like this always upset Davis; it was something he would never get used to. Sighing, he turned to the boy. 'Is this your father, Sam?'

Still standing by the window, the boy nodded. His face was blank and he gave the impression of being divorced from what was going on.

'He's dead. Did you know?'

Something crossed his face then. It was fleeting and Davis thought it may have been regret but it was gone so quickly, he really couldn't be sure. He came over and stood beside the policeman.

'He was alive when I went out a while ago,' he said dully. 'It must have just happened.' For a long moment he stared down at the lifeless body of the man who had been his father and then spat, quite deliberately, on the corpse. 'Fuck him, he was a complete waste of space – no loss to me or anyone else.'

The boy had clearly had a dreadful start in life but, even so, Davis was shocked by the coldness in his voice.

'Where's your mother, Sam?' he asked quietly.

He didn't reply at first and Davis was just about to repeat the question when the boy handed him a piece of paper. 'It was on the table,' he muttered. There was a disbelieving note in his voice when he spoke this time.

The policeman read the note. Short and to the point, it

read: 'sam, just don't need any more of this shite. You dads croaked and I don't want to be here no more. I never wanted u and I ain't going to waste any more of me life looking after u. The social can sort u out. mum.'

Although appallingly written, the note was clear enough. The boy's mother had deserted him and at just the time he needed her the most. Davis shook his head sadly – the selfishness that some human beings were capable of was a source of constant amazement to him. Putting his hand on Sam's shoulder comfortingly, he said softly, 'I'm, sorry lad.'

'Fuck her, she wasn't much better than he was,' came the angry retort. 'I don't need her any more than I needed him.'

'How old are you Sam – ten, eleven? You need someone to look after you. Your father's gone so it has to be your mother.'

The boy laughed bitterly. 'You have to be joking mate. She's done fuck all for me for at least the last two years.' The policeman said nothing, sensing he was about to open up a bit.

He continued, 'Before that she wasn't too bad. She fed me at least and got me clothes for school. Then she stopped and I've been looking after myself ever since.' Glaring at his father's body, he added. 'As for him …'

'Why did she stop?'

'You read the note – she never wanted me. I was always a pain-in-the-ass to her. It wasn't just that though; she was getting more and more like him – off her head on smack or pissed most of the time. She was a whore as well. Used to bring the dirty old bastards back here. They must have been desperate for a shag to go with her in a stinking shithole like this!'

Davis winced and not just at the language. This was a bad situation and he felt immense pity for the boy. 'So, you're telling me that you've been feeding yourself for the last two years by stealing. Is that right?'

'Mostly, apart from school dinners that is, and odd bits my mum brings in. He's provided nothing at all for as long as I can remember.'

'Clothing, toiletries, games, other stuff …?'

'Sam shrugged. 'Mister, whatever I need, I steal. There's been no other way for me for a long time now.'

Davis nodded. 'Okay.' He considered what he had to say next; he didn't want to worry or upset the boy any more than he already was. 'Sam, your father is dead. Now while I'm pretty sure that he killed himself with an over-dose, there is a possibility that somebody else, your mother maybe, had something to do with it. This means there will be a post-mortem carried out by a coroner to establish conclusively how he died. Also, I've caught you committing a crime and you've admitted to me that you've been involved in more. I also have to tell you that as a minor, I cannot leave you here alone in this flat. We will, of course, try and find your mother but, until we do, you'll have to go into care.'

'Fuck that, I can live on the street. I don't need help from anyone.' There was bravado in his voice and the policeman couldn't help but admire him for it.

He smiled sympathetically. 'That won't be necessary.

I'm going to pass you over to the social services for this area. They have a children's department who will find you somewhere to stay.'

The boy shrugged disinterestedly. 'Whatever.'

'I need to make some calls now, so I want you to stay here while I go outside. I'll just be a few minutes, okay?'

'Do what you like.'

'Don't worry, we'll soon have all this sorted out.' Going out, Davis closed the door behind him. The air in the stairwell was like fresh Arctic air in comparison to the fetid atmosphere in the flat. He could have made his calls while in there but it was a good excuse to get out of the stinking place for a few minutes.

Pacing up and down, he made a series of phone calls. His first was to the coroner for the southern district of Greater London. Unlike most of the council's departments, the coroner's office was on the ball and he knew it would just be a short time before the body was removed and taken away for the post-mortem.

His second call was to the Safeguarding Children Board department of Croydon Social Services. Getting through to a rather abrupt woman, Davis explained that he had a boy in need of shelter and asked that they find him somewhere to stay as a matter of urgency. She promised she would get it organised asap and send someone over to collect him.

He then phoned the police station and reported the situation. Davis was instructed to remain at the flat until the body had been removed and the social services had collected Sam.

An hour later, two men from the coroner's office arrived with a body bag. Placing the body of John Clark inside, they zipped it up, loaded it on to a stretcher and, without further ado, departed.

Davis watched Sam while this was going on and had felt distinctly sad at the boy's apparent lack of interest. He spent the entire time seated at the table staring impassively out of the window. Davis couldn't help but feel a touch of sadness for the father as well; such an ignominious way to go.

When the coroner's men had gone, he pulled a chair over and sat down next to the boy. 'Sam, I want you to listen to me carefully. The social services will be coming for you soon and a lot depends on how you behave with them. Don't cause them any trouble. Just keep your head down and do what they tell you. You understand what I'm saying?'

The boy nodded.

'Okay, pack a bag with whatever you are likely to need. You'll get just the bare essentials at the care home.'

Half an hour later, the man from social services arrived. Wrinkling his nose as he walked in, he flashed his ID card at Davis and introduced himself as Geoff. When the policeman had appraised him of the situation, he turned to Sam who was standing there awkwardly, a packed haversack at his feet, and said in a brusque voice, 'Come on then, let's be having you.'

Picking up the haversack, Sam made his way to the door. About to go out, he suddenly stopped and looked back at the policeman. 'Thanks mister.'

Davis was touched – it wasn't often that he got any appreciation for his efforts. 'I'm not sure you should be thanking me; it could be that your troubles are just beginning,' he muttered to himself.

Standing to the side of the KFC shop, the two men watched the commuter pull out his wallet, pay for his food and then tuck the wallet back inside his jacket pocket. As he walked away toward the exit of Charing Cross Underground Station, they went into action, one moving ahead of him and the other falling in behind.

When they were both in position, the man in front dropped a newspaper to the ground, stopped suddenly and bent down to pick it up. Too close to stop, the commuter walked straight into the back of him. With the mark thus distracted, the man behind stepped up and took the wallet from his inside pocket.

'What the hell are you doing?' the commuter said irritably.

'Sorry mate. I was just picking up my paper.'

'Well, be a bit more careful.' Pushing past impatiently, the commuter went on his way completely unaware he had just fallen victim to the classic 'sandwich' manoeuvre. His attention fixed on the man he'd collided with, he hadn't noticed the one behind him. It would be lunch time before he realised his wallet was missing.

Shaking his head disgruntledly for the benefit of the security cameras, the decoy picked up his newspaper and walked out onto Trafalgar Square where he waited for his accomplice to catch up with him.

Home to the iconic Nelson's Column, the Square was within walking distance of major London tourist attractions such as Somerset House, the National Portrait Gallery, St James's Park, Big Ben and the Houses of Parliament. This made it a positive mecca for pickpockets. Along with the Pantheon in Rome, Charles Street in Prague and Las Ramblas in Barcelona, Trafalgar Square was one of the most likely areas in Europe for a tourist to have his/her pocket picked.

He didn't need to ask how it had gone – Bernie never missed. The two men wandered over to a "Beware of Pickpockets" sign and stood to one side of it. Pulling out a pack of cigarettes, Bernie passed one across to his companion, Charlie, and they stood smoking while watching the crowds of tourists. To the casual observer, they could have been tourists themselves, dressed as they were in jeans, t-shirts and baseball caps. Once it wouldn't have mattered so much but with closed circuit television cameras all over the place now, these days it was essential to blend in.

It was a good place to spot potential marks. Many people, on seeing the sign, would instinctively pat the pocket holding their wallet or purse to check it was still there. The watching pickpockets then knew exactly where it was.

'There.' Flicking his cigarette away, Bernie pointed to a woman buying an ice cream. He had seen her put her purse in her shoulder bag and sling it back over her shoulder. She was a sitting duck.

Ambling across, he stopped a couple of metres in front of her where she couldn't help but see him. Pulling out a map, Bernie studied it for a moment before shaking his head as though confused. Looking up, he caught the woman's eye and, putting on his best American accent, asked, 'Excuse me ma'am, could you show me the way to the London Eye.' He held the map out so she could see it.

The woman didn't suspect a thing. 'Yes, of course.' Pointing over to the southeast corner of the Square, she said, 'Go down Northumberland Avenue and then across the Hungerford footbridge. It's about a mile or so – you can't miss it.'

As she was talking, Charlie walked up behind her and removed the purse from her bag without breaking stride. Within seconds, he had vanished into the crowds thronging the Square.

Bernie nodded at the woman. 'I'm indebted to you ma'am. Enjoy your ice cream.'

'Thank you, I will.' Flashing him a cheery smile, she went on her way.

Minutes later, the two pickpockets met up again at the base of Nelsons Column. Bernie watched his pal approach with some concern. In his mid-sixties, Charlie looked quite a lot older. His thinning hair and beard were snow white, his frame thin and bony, and he had a limp that was getting quite bad. Even worse, the fingers of his good hand were becoming arthritic and Bernie couldn't help but wonder how much longer he would be able to carry on. It had got to the stage now where he was having to do most of the lifting while Charlie did the diversions.

'I think I'll call it a day. Fucking leg's playing me up something wicked,' Charlie complained as he came up to Bernie.

'Okay. Let's grab a pint and divvy up.' Bernie hid his irritation. Conditions were ideal, the tourists were out in force and money was there for the taking. Perhaps he'd come back later after seeing Charlie off. Operating as an individual meant he would have to be a lot more selective in choice of mark, and it was riskier, but days like this were too good to pass up.

Stopping at the nearest pub, they took their drinks over to a table. The place was quiet inside; most of the customers sitting in the beer garden taking advantage of the fine weather.

'Let's see what we've got then.' Charlie put the woman's purse on the table and Bernie added three wallets he'd taken earlier. Emptying them, Charlie sorted the notes into denominations before doing a tally. 'Four hundred and twenty pounds. Not bad for two and a half hours work,' he declared.

Bernie could see his partner was making an effort to be upbeat. He looked tired and it was obvious he was in pain from his gammy leg. While he sympathised, Bernie was also concerned for himself. What with the leg and arthritic fingers, his partner was losing his edge and it was just a question of time before he made a serious mistake and got them both caught.

Bernie knew he was going to have to end their long-running partnership soon. It was something he wasn't looking forward to.

At the top of the stairs, Geoff gestured to Sam that he should go first. The man was overweight and Sam took a perverse pleasure in skipping nimbly down the stairs. He missed the hard, unfriendly glare that the man directed at the back of his head as he struggled to keep up. By the time they'd reached the bottom, he was red in the face and not in a good humour.

Stepping up behind him, the social services man gripped his shoulder firmly. 'Don't cause me any trouble boy.' He was obviously half-expecting Sam to try and do a runner.

Waiting at the pavement outside was a car. As soon as he saw them appear, the driver started the engine. Opening the rear door, Geoff pushed Sam inside and then climbed in beside him.

Sam's mind was in overdrive. It had been a hell of a day and there was more to come, he knew. And from what the policeman had said about keeping his head down, it wasn't necessarily anything for the better! Plus, thanks to his parents' dealings with state officialdom, he knew enough to not want to be in its hands anyway. He had to escape, and he had more chance of succeeding if he did it before they got to wherever he was being taken. A plan formed in his mind.

After ten minutes or so, he yawned, feigning tiredness. 'How long before we get there?'

Geoff shook his head irritably. 'At this rate, we'll be at least another hour.' They were in the middle of the London rush hour and the traffic was, quite literally, crawling along.

Sam grunted and laid has head against the seat, closing his eyes. After a few minutes, he let his head slump away from Geoff, making it difficult for the man to see if his eyes were open or closed.

Initially, Geoff was suspicious and kept glancing at him. He wasn't too sure of this boy – he had an edgy attitude that spelled possible trouble. Geoff didn't like kids that gave him trouble. It wasn't long though before, with his charge apparently asleep, he relaxed and buried his head in his phone.

It was a good fifteen minutes later when Sam made his move. The car had stopped at a red light. He had no idea what part of London they were in; only that the pavement on his side was crowded and thus ideal for losing himself in. As stealthily as he could, he opened the door just enough to allow him to slip out. Looking at Geoff from the corner of his eye, he saw the man was still engrossed with his phone.

Easing himself through the gap, Sam took off as fast as his legs would carry him. He was five metres away and disappearing into the crowd when he heard Geoff's angry bellow. 'Stop that boy.'

He would have made it easily if he hadn't, for the second time that day, had the incredible misfortune to run straight into a policeman. Head down and already out of sight from the social services man, he was beetling down the pavement when he ran smack into an unyielding figure dressed in blue. Looking up, Sam saw that rarest of sights in modern-day Britain – a policeman on the beat. If he'd have had the time, he would have shaken his head in disbelief. Pulling back, he tried to dodge round the man but the policeman reached out and grabbed his arm.

'What's your hurry then?' he enquired. 'Up to no-good, by any chance?'

Sam was just opening his mouth to answer, when Geoff arrived on the scene. 'Well done. The little sod was trying to escape.'

The policeman eyed him suspiciously. 'And who might you be?'

The council man fished out his ID. 'I'm from the social services. I'm taking this boy to a care home. He's just done a runner from the car as we were stopped at the lights over there.' Geoff jerked his thumb over his left shoulder.

'Hmm.' The policeman didn't seem convinced. 'Is what this man says right lad?'

For a second or two, Sam considered denying it but a moment's thought told him there really wasn't anything to be gained by doing so. He would be taken to the police station while checks were made but, eventually, he would find himself back where he was now – in the care of the council.

He sighed, 'Yeah.'

'Why were you trying to get away from him?' The policeman was still unsure.

Sam couldn't think of anything useful to say so he just stared at the ground.

'This is ridiculous.' Geoff was getting angry. 'I've explained the situation. Now let us get on our way.'

The policeman looked at him unenthusiastically before nodding curtly. He obviously wasn't much taken with the social services man. Gazing down at Sam, he said, 'Good luck,' and then resumed his patrol, leaving Geoff glaring indignantly after him.

They were soon back in the car and on their way. Sam was now resigned to what was happening. He wasn't going to escape again that was for sure, as Geoff was watching him like a hawk now.

Three quarters of an hour later, the car swung into a wide avenue lined with red brick houses on either side. About two-thirds of the way down, they entered the driveway of an enormous detached Victorian house. Above the large double-fronted door, there was a sign that read: "Shirley Heights Boys Home".

Geoff shook his arm roughly. 'Come on, we're here.'

Getting out reluctantly, Sam saw the driver was already out and blocking him in case he made another run for it. Standing at the foot of the steps that led to the door, he gazed up at the imposing three-storey building nervously; he had a distinct feeling he wasn't going to like the place.

Inside was a reception area with a rather sour faced woman seated behind a desk. Putting her phone down with obvious reluctance, she looked Sam up and down disparagingly as he approached.

'What have we got here then?' Her manner was casual, disinterested.

'Hello Sylvie.' Geoff looked at his clipboard. 'His name is Sam Clark. Apparently, the father's a druggie – killed himself with an overdose earlier today, and the mother, another druggie, has cleared off and left him to fend for himself. The usual stuff.' He shrugged as if to say, 'What can you do?' There wasn't the faintest trace of sympathy in his voice.

Sylvie nodded and pushed a sheet of paper across the desk. 'Fill in the admissions form and we'll get him sorted out.'

A few minutes later Geoff handed the completed form back to her. 'That's me done. I'll be off now.' With that he departed, not sparing Sam so much as a glance.

The woman pressed a button on the desktop. 'Someone will be along in a minute to get you.' Picking her phone up again, she proceeded to ignore him completely.

Half an hour later, a door to the side of the reception room opened and a short, very fat, man waddled through. Approaching Sam who was pacing up and down nervously, he gestured at his bag and said in a gruff voice, 'I'm Simon. Pick up your stuff and follow me.' Turning on his heel, he waddled back the way he had come. Sam followed him up a flight of stairs and into a corridor with numbered doors every few metres on either side. It resembled nothing so much as a prison and his feeling of apprehension grew.

The corridor was dimly lit and he could see light showing under most of the doors. Simon stopped at one about halfway down. 'This is your room. You'll be woken at 6.30am and breakfast is at 7.00am. Dinner is at 6.00pm. Tomorrow, you'll have an assessment so that a suitable care plan for you can be worked out.' The speech was short and to the point.

Opening the door, he ushered Sam inside. Not speaking another word, he then closed and locked it from the outside, leaving the boy alone in his new surroundings.

Sam looked around curiously. The room was small with an old fashioned and uncomfortable looking iron bed and a chest of drawers along one wall. Over the bed was a window. There was also a small table and single chair and, alongside the far wall, a TV set on a stand. Through an open door at the side of the room, he could see a small bathroom. Going in, he saw a toilet, shower and basin. Above the basin was a shattered mirror. He pulled a face at the sight – the bathroom mirror at the flat had been just the same.

Overall, the accommodation was just about as basic and uninspiring as it could possibly be. It was, however, warm and clean – luxuries he had not experienced for a long time. He also had it entirely to himself – no drug-addled father, no drug dealers pushing their killer wares, no drunken mother ranting and raving in an alcohol-induced rage, no strange "gentlemen" being entertained in her bedroom. While he had known he was not going to miss 608 Cromwell House one iota, Sam had been apprehensive at what was going to replace it. Having seen it now, basic as it was, he was feeling a bit happier.

He switched the TV set on. The picture was a bit fuzzy but was, nevertheless, watchable. The TV in the flat had been put out of action when his father had thrown a bottle at it, his befuddled mind terrified that he was about to be attacked by a lion that happened to be on the screen. That had been at least a year ago and Sam hadn't watched television since.

Sitting on the bed, he flicked through the channels until he found something to watch. It wasn't long though before the day's events began to catch up with him and he nodded off.

The next morning, Sam was awakened by a loud klaxon blaring in the corridor outside. Wondering what the hell today was going to bring, he got washed and dressed. With nothing to do, he then sat down in the chair and waited. It was a good three quarters of an hour later when a key rattled in the door and it opened to reveal Simon standing there. Jerking his head, the fat man said, 'Come on, I'll take you to breakfast. You'll be a bit late – I overslept.' There was no apology and his voice was as dull and robotic as it had been the previous evening.

As they walked down the corridor, Sam had to match his step to that of the slow-moving Simon. He'd been too tired last night to take much notice but now he could see just how enormously fat the man really was. He quite literally lumbered along, taking small shuffling steps, all the while breathing heavily. Sam had never seen anyone like him.

After what seemed an eternity, they reached the end of the corridor and turned to the right. A few metres further down was a set of double doors with the legend "Dining Room" in faded letters above. Pushing the door open, Simon said, 'I'll be back for you at half past.'

Glancing at his watch, Sam saw that gave him fifteen minutes to get and eat his breakfast. Entering, he stood and looked around for a moment to get his bearings. It was a large room with a number of tables, all of which were occupied by boys of various ages. At a quick estimate there were about thirty of them. The breakfast fare was laid out on a long table along the far wall. Suddenly aware of how ravenous he was, he made his way over and loaded a plate with as much bacon, egg, sausage and beans as it could hold. There was an empty seat at a nearby table and, sitting down, he proceeded to tuck in ignoring his table companions completely.

He was two-thirds of the way through it when an amused voice to his left spoke. 'You eat as though you haven't seen food for a week.'

Sam glanced at the speaker. He was a good-looking lad about the same age, and he had an amused look on his face.

Chewing on a mouthful of sausage, Sam just nodded.

'You must have come in last night; I didn't see you around yesterday.' He seemed curious.

'Yesterday evening. I was so knackered I went straight to sleep.'

The boy hesitated for a moment and then said, 'I'm Fred.'

'Sam. You been here long?' He knew virtually nothing about the place and, while he wasn't really in the mood for conversation, this was a good opportunity to find out.

'Seven months now.'

'What happens here?'

'This is a place for people who have nowhere to go. They give you a room, something to eat in the morning, a bus ride to school and back, something to eat at night and fuck all else.' Fred didn't sound as though he was particularly enamoured. 'And, if you're lucky, you get left alone by the bastards who run it. If you're not ...' his voice tailed off.

Sam glanced at him curiously. 'What do you mean?'

His companion looked around, obviously not wanting to be overheard. 'Listen mate, you have to keep your head down in this place. For starters, watch out for that guy over there,' he nodded over towards a door that Sam guessed led to the kitchen. Standing next to it was a tall, well-built man of about fifty, his eyes continuously sweeping the room and its inhabitants. He hadn't noticed him before.

Fred continued. 'His name's Stan Dixon – ex army. He's one of the staff; goes around keeping an eye on things. He's got eyes like a hawk and will pull you up for anything. If he does, whatever you do, don't argue with him, just do what he tells you to. Then there's Sylvie – she's the one at the reception desk. Be careful what you say in front of her, she reports everything she hears to the guvnor upstairs, and he's someone you really don't want to meet.'

'Why don't I want to meet him? Who is he anyway?'

'His name is Thomas Lloyd and he's a real nasty bastard. He's the top man in this place.'

'Nasty in what way?'

Fred was just opening his mouth to answer when the man Dixon suddenly left his post by the kitchen door and came striding over towards them. His eyes were narrowed slightly as though he was suspicious about something.

Stopping by Sam, he barked, 'I take it you're the one who came in last night. Clark, is that right?'

Sam nodded.

'Answer me when I speak to you.' The man's manner was aggressive, intimidating.

Sam wasn't in the mood for agro. Looking down at the table, he mumbled, 'I'm sorry Sir. Yes, I did come in last night.'

'That's more like it. I'm in charge around here and you'll do well not to forget it.' Switching his attention to Fred, he snapped, 'What have you been telling this lad, Hancock?'

'He's new here Mr Dixon. I've just been explaining how things work in this place. That's all, honest.'

'Hmm.' Dixon gave Fred a hard stare before turning and going back to his station by the kitchen door.

'Dickhead,' Fred muttered contemptuously. As he spoke, a klaxon went off. 'Well that's breakfast finished.' Pushing his chair back, he got up from the table.

Looking around, Sam saw everyone else was getting up as well. 'So, what happens now?' he asked.

'For us,' Fred indicated the other boys with a sweep of his arm, 'it's back to our rooms, get our school things together and then assemble outside and wait for the school buses. For you, I don't know – whatever they've told you. See you later perhaps.'

Sam watched as the boy headed for the door. He was aware that Fred hadn't yet told him what the problem was with the head, Thomas Lloyd. Shrugging, he stuffed the last bit of sausage into his mouth. It may have been rushed but it was still the best breakfast he'd eaten in a long time. He was wondering what to do next when the door opened and Simon popped his head round.

'There you are Clark. Come on, I'll take you back to your room.'

Adjusting himself to Simon's snail pace as they went down the corridor, he asked, 'Why can't I go back by my-self? I know where it is.'

The man brandished a key. 'Because I've got the key. This is your first day here and you have to be examined by a doctor. Then you will be assessed by a care worker to establish if you have any special needs. After that, I'll take you round to familiarise you with the place. When all that's been done and we are happy with you and you are happy with us, you will be given the key to your room. But until then, we have to keep a close eye on you. It's just the rules, okay?

Sam nodded resignedly.

Simon locked him in and then disappeared. The doctor

came at 10.30 and examined Sam. He was of a foreign nationality and Sam struggled to understand much of what he said. When he'd finished, the guy just packed his stuff away and left without bothering to tell him anything. Simon had locked him in again.

He then surfed channels on the TV until early afternoon when Simon reappeared with a plate of burger and chips. The fat man stayed for a few minutes and, for the first time, chatted quite amiably while Sam wolfed down his food. The burger was greasy and the chips thin and hard but he enjoyed them nevertheless.

The care worker arrived mid-afternoon. Armed with the inevitable clipboard, she asked a series of questions that she said would enable her to get him the best possible care. He had the impression she was genuine and meant well, so he answered as best he could. Then he was locked in yet again.

The rest of the afternoon stretched interminably and, by the time Simon reappeared to take him to the evening meal, Sam was in a fractious and irritable mood.

Once again, Simon got him to the dining room late and Sam found that the rest of the boys were already seated and tucking in. There were just a couple of other boys at the buffet table filling their plates. Reaching across to help himself to a slice of pizza, he inadvertently brushed against the one standing next to him.

Turning around, the boy glared at Sam and spat, 'Don't push me you little fuck.' There was something of the night about him – his features were ugly and brutish, half his teeth were missing and there was a long scar running down the left side of his face. Somewhat incongruously, he had a magnificent mane of ginger hair tied back in a long ponytail.

Sam wasn't in the mood for confrontation; besides which the boy was older and considerably bigger. Hiding his irritation, he just nodded and said in a quiet voice, 'Sorry.' He held the boy's stare though.

'Touch me again and I'll rip your fucking head off.' With that the oaf turned away. Sam shook his head and carried on filling his plate. Standing at the end of the buffet table, he looked for a place to sit. As luck would have it, the only empty seat was next to the boy with the ginger hair.

He was too hungry to care. Shrugging, he went over and sat down. Nevertheless, he was careful not to intrude on Ginger's space – he didn't want any further trouble. As he ate, Sam noticed that while there was a lot of banter between the other boys at the table, Ginger didn't join in. Instead he just sat there wolfing his food down. His table manners were appalling.

Sam was halfway through his dinner when he became aware that the boy had stopped eating and was staring fixedly at him. It was unsettling but he forced himself to ignore him and kept on eating. Quickly though, the table fell silent and he could see the other boys were all looking at Ginger expectantly.

Suddenly, Sam had had enough. Looking at him, he snapped, 'What?'

'I don't like you. Fuck off.' Ginger's coarse features were twisted, his voice menacing.

'I've not finished eating. When I have, I'll be happy to fuck off. Okay?' To the other boys, he appeared completely unperturbed. He added, 'By the way, I don't like you either.'

Immediately on saying this, he heard one of his table companions suck in his breath while another chuckled. Glancing round, he saw they were all watching intently.

Sam turned and stared Ginger full in the face. For a few moments the oaf just glared menacingly back at him. Then he hawked, leaned forward and spat on to Sam's plate. Sitting back, he folded his arms and a mirthless grin spread across his face. It was a clear challenge. 'What are you going to do about that?'

It was the straw that broke the camel's back. Sam had just endured the worst twenty-four hours of his life. He was worried, miserable, upset, frustrated, angry at the world and his response was instantaneous and brutal. Ginger had just finished folding his arms when Sam's left arm shot out and the palm of his hand opened behind Ginger's head. Dragging it forward and down, he smashed it into the boy's dinner plate with all the force he could muster. The plate, made of thin cheap china, shattered and Sam ground his face into the sharp-edged pieces before yanking his head viciously back up.

There were gasps, not just from their table, but from around the entire room at the resulting sight. Ginger's face was covered in a gruesome looking layer comprised of blood from his shattered nose, and sauce and bits of pasta from his food. There were several deep cuts from the shards of broken plate and blood from these dripped down his chin and on to his shirt.

Sam wasn't finished yet – he was filled with a cold rage that could be released in one way only. Retaining his grip on the boy's long ginger locks, he stood and heaved him backwards so both he and the chair crashed to the floor. Absolutely shell-shocked, the yob lay there groaning piteously.

Sam stared down at him contemptuously, then drew his boot back and crashed it into Ginger's groin, eliciting a scream of pure agony. The dining room was deathly quiet now and the only sounds in it were those coming from the stricken boy – bloody snuffles and a horrible whimpering. His opponent absolutely helpless, Sam straddled him and began raining blows into his face. It was brutal but from the gleeful encouragement that came from the assembled onlookers, such as: 'Smash the bastard's face in,' 'Give him one for me,' 'Nice one mate,' it was clear that Ginger had few, if any, friends in the care home.

Seconds later, the overseer, Mr Dixon, came charging into the room from the direction of the kitchen. He'd been having a smoke by the back door when Ginger's dreadful scream had alerted him. The scene that greeted him brought him skidding to a halt, literally gaping in astonishment. He'd seen some sights in his days in the army and the ginger-haired boy's battered and bloodied face was as gruesome as any of them. His astonishment was twofold: first the ferocity displayed by the new boy and, second, the fact that he was administering the beating to Jason Brown who was not only much older but was feared by all the other boys as a hard case to be avoided. Indeed, the care home staff themselves were wary of him.

Dixon detested the foul mouthed, ill-mannered lout and so for a moment was sorely tempted to stand back and let the beating continue a bit longer. It was more than his job was worth though, so with some regret he grabbed Sam's collar and pulled him away.

Staring down, he said coldly, 'Well Brown, it seems you've met your match at last.' From past experiences with him, Dixon was in no doubt that he had instigated the incident. Turning to the nearest onlooker, he said, 'Nip to the front desk Tompkins and tell Mrs Giles to phone for a doctor. Then find Mr Gardiner and tell him to get over here.'

Dixon looked at the crush of boys crowding round and gawping at the poleaxed Jason Brown. Raising his voice so he could be heard above the excited babble, he demanded, 'Now then, I want to know exactly what happened.'

Minutes later, Simon Gardner entered the room and whistled in amazement at the sight of Jason Brown on the floor, his face covered in blood.

'Take Clark back to his room please Mr Gardner,' Dixon ordered.

An hour later, Sam was stretched out on his bed and replaying the incident with Jason Brown in his head for the umpteenth time. While well pleased with the way he'd put him in his place, he was more than a little concerned at what the incident might lead to. He was uncomfortably aware that while in this place, he was completely at the mercy of the people who ran it. He was cursing himself for a fool – he should have ignored Brown – the prat would have got fed up after a while and just gone away, when there was a sharp rap at the door. Getting off the bed, he opened it to see Dixon standing in the corridor.

'Come on Clark, someone wants to see you.' He sounded almost apologetic.

'The guvnor I suppose.' There was resignation in Sam's voice.

Dixon just nodded – he didn't seem very happy.

It wasn't long before they were standing outside the manager's office. Dixon knocked on the door.

'Come in,' a deep voice called out.

Placing his hand on Sam's shoulder, Dixon gently ushered him inside. His manner was sympathetic, in sharp contrast to the cold brusqueness of the previous day. It made Sam nervous; it was as though the man knew something he didn't.

Seated behind a large wooden desk facing the door was the man Sam presumed to be Thomas Lloyd. He was a strange looking individual, with a completely bald head, long lean face, sharp pointed nose and an unkempt beard. It was his eyes that held Sam's attention though. There was something dark and calculating in them. All-in-all, an unnerving individual, and that was before he'd spoken a word.

Bringing him to a stop in front of the desk, Dixon announced, 'Sam Clark, Sir.' His voice was neutral, his face expressionless.

'Thank you, Mr Dixon. I'll take it from here,' Lloyd said

quietly. Waiting until the man had departed, he leaned back in his chair and took a long, leisurely look at the boy standing in front of him. Of average height and build for his age, physically, there was nothing unusual about him. However, unlike most of the boys who had to face Lloyd for the first time, he didn't seem particularly worried or concerned at finding himself hauled before the head man on his first full day in the home.

Lloyd had just read the case file on Clark and while it was sketchy on detail, it did highlight the appalling start to life he had suffered. Lloyd had seen hundreds of such boys pass through the care home over the years and had been expecting to see an under-nourished, frightened and confused youth. Instead, he was looking at someone who was none of these things.

He also couldn't help but notice that Clark was an exceptionally good-looking lad with startling blue eyes, features that were even and well formed, and a thick mop of jet-black hair. Just the way he liked them, in fact.

Picking up a sheet of typewritten paper from the desk, Lloyd frowned at Sam. 'This is the report Mr Dixon has given me regarding the incident in the dining room. I have to tell you young man, I am not impressed. You've been here less than twenty-four hours and already you're causing trouble. Brawling like a thug in the dining room, or anywhere else for that matter, is not tolerated in this establishment. From the report, it appears you were the one who started the fight. What do you have to say?'

Actually, Dixon had said nothing of the sort. He'd admitted he was out of the room at the time and so missed the start of the confrontation. He'd told Lloyd that according to the other boys, it was Brown who had provoked Clark. The new boy had simply responded to the provocation, albeit in a rather brutal fashion.

Lloyd had a motive for pretending otherwise though. He wanted to frighten the boy to shake the confidence and defiance out of him so that he would be easier to handle and manipulate. With most boys it wasn't necessary to do this – they were usually already nervous as hell. He had a feeling this one wasn't going to be so easy, however.

Standing there facing the manager's scrutiny, beneath his calm exterior, Sam was apprehensive. The man sitting behind the desk bothered him greatly. He couldn't really say why but his instincts were telling him that there was something bad going on here. But what?

'No, it wasn't me that started it. He was bullying me and then he spat in my food. What was I supposed to do?' he said defiantly.

'If that's true, you should have reported it to Mr Dixon, not attack Brown. But it's not true is it? It was you who started the fight. Now you're trying to lie your way out of trouble. Well, I'm afraid it's not going to work.'

Throwing Dixon's report down on the desk angrily, Lloyd continued accusingly. 'Brown has had to be taken to hospital and I'm told he has serious injuries. You've committed a criminal assault and by rights I should report you to the police.' Staring coldly at the boy standing in front of him, he waited for a reaction. There was threat in his manner now.

Sam was thinking fast. While he really couldn't see the police taking any notice of a punch-up between two boys, he couldn't be sure. After all, he had given the prat a good beating and, if he really was in hospital with injuries, it may be that the police *would* take an interest. There was enough shit in his life at the moment as it was, and he didn't need any more. So he decided to adopt a more humble manner in the hope of placating the man in front of him.

Putting a worried look on his face, he mumbled, 'I'm very sorry sir. I hope he isn't too badly hurt. Please don't report me to the police. My father has just died and I don't know where my mother is or if I'll ever see her again. I'm just upset – that's why I lost it with him.' Letting his voice tail off, he stared miserably at the floor.

It was well said but Lloyd wasn't interested in it though. What did interest him was the fact that he now appeared to have the boy where he wanted him – worried and pleading. It triggered the old familiar stirring in his loins.

'It doesn't excuse what you've done but I am aware of what's happened with your mother and father,' he said in a more understanding tone. 'And yes, of course, I do appreciate how difficult your situation is at the moment. For that reason, I am prepared to overlook the incident and put this in the bin.' Picking up the sheet of paper from his desk, he held it over the waste basket.

With no knowledge of the man, Sam had no way of knowing how badly he was being deceived. The care home manager was lying – he couldn't have cared less about Sam's situation. There was only one thing on his mind.

Lloyd brandished the report. 'But before I do, I want you to do something for me.' There was something strange in his voice as he said, 'Come round here.'

Sam didn't have a clue what the man wanted. However, he did as he was asked. As he rounded the side of the desk, Lloyd pushed his wheeled chair back and swivelled so he was facing the boy. To Sam's utter bemusement, he saw the man was holding his exposed penis.

He stopped abruptly – he couldn't believe what he was seeing. Given all that had happened to him in the last twenty-four hours or so, the thought crossed his mind that he was going mad.

Seeing his confusion, Lloyd chuckled. It wasn't a pleasant sound. Gesturing at his erect cock, he said, 'Here's the deal boy. I want you to hold my willy and rub it like this.' Wanking himself briefly with his right hand, he gave Sam a quick demonstration. 'And don't stop until I tell you to.'

Completely nonplussed by what was happening, Sam just stood there, not knowing how to react.

'If you don't, this,' Lloyd waved the report, 'will be sent to the police first thing tomorrow morning. You know what will happen then.'

They stared at each other for a few moments before Sam suddenly found his voice, 'Fuck off you dirty old bastard. Report me then, I bet the cops will be more interested in what goes on in this place.'

Lloyd looked at the boy and laughed loudly. 'You really think they will take any notice of anything a filthy street urchin like you has to say?' Turning his head, he bawled, 'Gardiner, get in here.'

A door on the right-hand side of the office opened immediately and in waddled the fat man, Simon. 'Giving you trouble boss?' he asked with a chuckle.

Lloyd grinned mirthlessly. 'He thinks he is. All he's doing though is making things worse for himself, as he will discover in due course.' He got to his feet, his erect penis jutting out in front of him.

'Hold the little shit down.'

'With pleasure.' Simon crossed the room and grabbed Sam roughly by the shoulders. Spinning him round, he forced the boy down across the desk. This was as involved as the fat man ever got. A voyeur, he was content to just watch through a spyhole in the wall that divided the two rooms. It was only when the boss couldn't frighten them into doing what he wanted that he was called on to lend a hand.

Sam struggled as hard as he could but had no chance against the enormous weight that was pinning him face down to the desk. Eager hands pulled at his jeans and underpants before caressing his naked behind. He squirmed and wriggled in horror at what was happening to him but could do nothing to prevent it. Mercifully, it was only a few minutes before it was over – Lloyd gave a grunt and pulled away. The weight was suddenly lifted from Sam but instead of getting up, he remained spread-eagled across the desk, not moving. The brutality of it had shocked him rigid.

'Come on, stand up, you're not getting any more if

that's what you're waiting for.' From behind him, Simon laughed heartlessly.

Standing up, Sam reached down and pulled up his clothes. Then he just stood numbly waiting for whatever was going to happen next.

Lloyd spoke. 'I told you what I wanted you to do and you refused. I also told you what would happen if you didn't. So, first thing tomorrow morning, I will be contacting the police and informing them of your brutal assault on Jason Brown. You will almost certainly be put in a young offender's institution and I wish you luck with that.' He made it sound as though Sam was giving him no choice and that he would be doing it reluctantly.

It was a nasty lie designed purely to worry the boy. He actually had no intention to reporting him to the police. They wouldn't be interested as he well knew. They had enough on their hands already catching real criminals to waste time on a ten year-old juvenile. Not only was he a paedophile, Lloyd also enjoyed mental cruelty and got a kick out of seeing the little bastards, as he saw them, frightened and upset.

And it worked all too well. Not only was Sam in considerable pain and shock from Lloyd's brutal sexual assault, he now also had the added worry of wondering what was to happen to him next. Simply incapable of speech, he just stood there in a daze.

'All right Mr Gardiner, take him back to his room and lock him in.' Lloyd watched as Simon pushed Sam none too gently towards the door. When they had gone, he sat back in his chair with a smile and relived the rape in his mind. Little did he know the price he would one day pay for it.

Stumbling down the corridor with the fat man pushing him along, Sam suddenly came to his senses. The manager's threat to report him to the police had him worried. It probably wasn't true but it was a risk he couldn't take. Nor could he risk any more of what had just happened to him. There was nothing for it, he realised – he had to escape from the home. And, as he was about to be locked in his room, the time to do it was right now. The only thing stopping him was Simon.

As they walked, ahead of them, Sam saw the staircase that led down to the ground floor approaching. Immediately, a way of incapacitating the fat man occurred to him. As he reached the staircase, he began to stagger from side to side and then collapsed right at the head of the stairs. Rolling on to his back, he clutched at himself and groaned piteously as though in great pain.

Coming up behind, Simon stood and stared down at him uncertainly. 'What's the matter with you?' There was suspicion in his voice. A moment ago the boy had seemed fine and now, all of a sudden, he appeared to be at deaths door.

Sam groaned again and then, clutching at his stomach, cried out as though in mortal pain. It was a convincing performance. Now certain something was amiss, Simon bent down to get a better look. As he did so, his great bulk put him off balance and Sam suddenly reached up, grabbed the front of his shirt, and heaved him forward and down the stairs.

Simon cried out as he tumbled down and crashed to the bottom. Running down behind him, Sam stopped and stared at the man as he lay there prone, praying he wasn't seriously injured. If he was, or God forbid, dead, then the police would definitely be taking an interest. Then, to his great relief, Simon groaned and began to stir. It was all Sam needed to see – he took off as fast as his legs would carry him. He knew there was a junction ahead and that the left turn would take him to the entrance lobby.

As he approached the lobby, he slowed his pace. Opening the door that led into it as quietly as he could, he peered round to the right where the reception desk was located. His heart leapt as he saw it was unattended. This was unexpected but very welcome. Nipping across the lobby, he pushed through the front door and hurried down the steps to the driveway. With a quick glance around to see if the coast was clear, he sprinted away.

Once out of sight of the care home, he slowed to a fast walk in order to not look suspicious. He had no idea of where he was other than the fact that it was in the borough of Camden. What he was sure of though, was that a search would be instigated for him almost immediately, and it might well involve the police. He had to drop completely out of sight and remain so for as long as it took for them to lose interest in him and give up.

As he walked, it suddenly dawned on him that for the first time in his life he was entirely alone. Possessions wise, he had nothing but the clothes on his back, he had no money and he had nowhere to call home. It was a chilling realisation.

Charlie Parker had had a good day. He'd spent the morning picking pockets in Piccadilly Circus and finished up with over £600 for his efforts. In the afternoon, he'd watched the London derby between Spurs and Arsenal at White Hart Lane and, as a lifelong Spurs supporter, had been thrilled when his side ran out 3-2 winners. On his way home from the match, he'd called in at the Bricklayers Arms for a celebratory pint.

He was just coming out of the pub when a taxi pulled over to the side of the road just a few metres away. Literally under his nose, he couldn't fail to see the passenger get out, pull his wallet out of a back pocket, pay the driver and then stuff the wallet back in the same pocket.

Never one to pass up an opportunity, Charlie was about to fall in behind the man when a scruffy looking boy darted up in front of him. What happened next was enough to make the professional in Charlie wince. There was absolutely no finesse in how the boy did it – he simply plucked the wallet out of the man's pocket, turned and high-tailed it across the road, dodging the traffic as he went.

Seconds later, suddenly aware he had been robbed, the man shouted furiously, 'Oi, you little bastard. Come back here.' Desperately, his eyes tried to follow the thief as he weaved between the pedestrians on the opposite side of the road. The boy was far too fast for him though and was quickly out of sight. The man cursed long and loud before shrugging disgustedly and walking away down the street.

Charlie, however, had managed to keep the thief in view and saw him duck into a John Lewis department store. He was well acquainted with the store, having picked many a pocket there himself, and knew there was no rear exit from the place. The thief would have to come back out from the front.

Interested for some reason, he decided to wait and see what the boy did. When he came out some fifteen minutes later, Charlie nearly missed him – the lad had spent some of the loot on new jeans and a hoodie, which was pulled down around his face. As he walked swiftly away down the street, on an impulse, Charlie followed along behind.

The pace was fast and Charlie, with his bad leg, struggled to keep up. He was just beginning to wonder what the hell he was doing when the boy suddenly veered into a side street. Hurrying round the corner, Charlie was brought up short by the sight of the boy standing there facing him. There was an agitated look on his face. 'You've been following me. Who are you?' he demanded, 'the old bill?'

Charlie grimaced. 'You have to be joking. I don't need the police any more than you do.'

'Why are you following me then?'

Put on the spot, Charlie's mind was blank for a moment. It was a good question! Why was he following the boy? Spotting a coffee shop across the road, he said, 'Let me buy you a coffee and I'll explain.'

The boy just stared at him suspiciously.

'I'll buy you a doughnut as well.'

'You promise no funny stuff.'

It was an odd thing to say and set Charlie to wondering. 'You have my word young man.' Grinning, he added, 'for what that's worth.'

For some reason, it tickled the boy. With a half-smile, he said, 'Make it two doughnuts.'

Charlie chuckled, 'Go on then.'

When they were settled at a table, the lad wasted no time tucking into the food. As he wolfed it down, Charlie sat quietly, observing him. The boy was dirty, he was very thin and from the way he constantly looked around, clearly uneasy. Together with the fact he was having to steal, it all pointed to him being on the streets. Having been there himself, Charlie knew the signs.

Finishing the second doughnut, the boy looked across at Charlie. 'So, why were you following me?' He was disconcertingly direct.

'I may be able to help you.'

'What makes you think I need your help?'

Charlie took a moment before replying. This really wasn't any of his business and he knew he shouldn't be getting involved. But …!

'I think you are alone. Your parents are either dead, druggies or just buggered off. I think you're homeless and I know you are a thief. I saw you steal that man's wallet a while ago and then go and buy those clothes.'

Expecting a reaction of some sort – shock, fear, panic – Charlie was surprised at the way the boy just returned his gaze expressionlessly, giving absolutely nothing away.

After a moment, he said, 'Why would you want to help me? You don't know me; you know nothing about me.'

'You think so? I'm right though, aren't I? You *are* alone and homeless.'

Looking away, the boy stared unseeingly out the window, before muttering, 'Yeah, I've been sleeping rough for about a month now.'

'How old are you?'

'I'm ten.'

'Well, when I was ten, I was in exactly the same situation as you are. I had no family, nowhere to live and no money.' Charlie reached across and squeezed the boy's shoulder comfortingly. 'That's why I want to help you. I've been there myself, I understand better than anyone how crap your life is. I survived and, if you'll let me, I'll help you survive.' There was understanding and sympathy in his voice.

The boy stared at him searchingly and Charlie could see he desperately wanted to believe. Then he nodded hesitantly, and Charlie smiled. 'That's settled then,' he said gruffly. 'You can come and live with me. I don't have a big place – just a two-bed flat but you'll have a room of your own, a place to wash and you won't go hungry. That's all I promise though – the rest is up to you. Play fair with me and I'll play fair with you. Deal?'

The boy was still far from sure and Charlie really couldn't blame him. In his position, he would be thinking long and hard as well. There was a long silence before he muttered a wary, 'Deal.' Then, with a hint of wry humour, he added, 'If you're prepared to risk living with me, I'll take a chance on living with you.'

'I have a feeling we'll get along just fine,' the pickpocket laughed. 'I'm Charlie Parker. Who are you?'

'Sam Clark.'

'Okay Sam let's go. Thanks to you dragging me over half of London, we have a bloody long walk back to the flat.' Charlie laughed again. He didn't really know why but for some reason, he was really pleased that the boy had agreed to give it a go.

Thirty minutes later, they arrived at a tall tower block that was disturbingly similar to Cromwell House. Lounging aimlessly about the courtyard fronting the block were some distinctly shady looking characters and Sam could tell several of them were drugged up. The sight brought back the memory of his recently deceased father, thoughts of whom, not surprisingly, had all but vanished given what happened to him since. He shuddered involuntarily and, standing beside him, Charlie Parker misunderstood.

'Doesn't look too good from out here I know,' he muttered, casting a contemptuous glance at the youths, 'But it's a lot better inside. Come on, you'll see.'

Charlie's flat was situated on the tenth floor and, in terms of size and layout, was very similar to the flat that Sam had just recently been living in with his parents. It had two bedrooms, a living room, kitchen and bathroom. All the rooms were small. However, unlike Sam's parent's flat, this one was spotlessly clean and nicely furnished.

Having shown Sam the room that he was to sleep in, Charlie busied himself in the kitchen preparing something for their dinner. As he worked, he kept up a steady stream of friendly chatter and banter hoping to ease the boy's fears and help him to relax. And it worked. Sam soon realised that the man's friendliness was genuine, and, for some reason, he had taken a liking to him. He relaxed and began responding to his host. It wasn't long before Charlie was asking gently probing questions and Sam, to his surprise, found himself answering quite openly.

By the time they had finished their Spaghetti Bolognese dinner, Charlie had extracted the full story of Sam's miserable life to date. Falling quiet, he sat staring at his plate for a while before finally looking up and across the table at the boy.

'Listen Sam, this is what we're going to do. As I told you earlier, I know exactly what you have been through because I went through it myself. Because of that, and because I like you, I want to help. However, you need to understand a few things. Firstly, I'm not going to try and act like a parent. To be honest, I wouldn't know how. I won't be getting you up in the morning and telling you to go to bed at night, making sure you clean your teeth, take a bath and any of that stuff.'

Charlie had Sam's unswerving attention. He was now very aware of just how much his luck had changed for the better. Homeless and friendless just a few hours ago, now all of a sudden, he had both.

'Don't worry, you won't need to.'

Charlie nodded. 'Good. The next thing is your schooling. I don't know which school you were attending but you won't be going there anymore, or indeed any other school for that matter. If you were to, you ....'

'I know,' Sam interrupted. 'I'd be straight back in one of those fucking care homes.' Anger and disgust coursed through him as he remembered what the manager of the care home had done to him so recently.

Charlie had a good idea what he was thinking – the boy had told him about the assault. He moved on quickly to try and distract him from the unpleasant memory. 'Most of what they teach you in school is crap anyway. I've managed without it and so can you. All you really need to know is how to read, write and do sums. If you want me to, I can help you with those.'

'I might take you up on that.' Sam smiled at Charlie for the first time.

He nodded. 'Right then. I know all about you; now it's time you know something about me.' He grinned mischievously at Sam. 'You may change your mind about staying here when you do. The first thing you need to know is that I'm a thief and always have been.'

Sam raided his eyebrows in surprise. 'Really? What do you steal?'

'Cash mainly. I'm a pickpocket. That's why I noticed you earlier on this afternoon. That man you robbed in the street – I was just about to rob him myself but you beat me to it.' He narrowed his eyes playfully at Sam, 'How much was in the wallet by the way?'

Completely at ease now, Sam chuckled, 'One hundred and eighty-five pounds and some loose change. Never seen so much money in my life!'

'Fuck – if I'd been quicker off the mark that would have been mine,' Charlie shook his head in mock annoyance. 'I've got to tell you though, you were bloody lucky to get away with that. I'm going to have to teach you how to do it properly. Then I can just sit about and leave you to do all the work. What do you reckon?'

'Seriously? Will you really?' Sam's eyes were wide. He was perceptive enough to know that this was the best offer he'd had in his young life to date.

'Absolutely. You'll soon be in jail if I don't and I don't do jail visits.'

'When do we start?' Sam sounded as though he couldn't quite believe what was happening.

Charlie smiled. 'Tomorrow. I'm off out now to do some business, if you know what I mean.' He gave Sam a conspiratorial wink. 'Then I'll be in the pub with my mates until closing time.'

Looking at Sam seriously, he said. 'I've only got one key to the flat; I'll get another one cut for you tomorrow. Until then you'll have to stay in. So, make yourself at home – you're in charge until I get back.'

The boy understood that Charlie was really saying, 'I'm

trusting you, don't let me down.' Getting to his feet, he headed for the door. A quick 'see you later' and he was gone.

Alone with his thoughts now, Sam sat musing for a long time. He'd already virtually forgotten his parents – he'd hated them both and wasn't in the least sorry they were out of his life for good. With regard to what had taken place at the care home, he tried to be philosophical and put it to the back of his mind. It had happened, it couldn't be undone and so he may as well forget about it for now. There was a part of him though, that thought he might be meeting Thomas Lloyd again, and this time with a different outcome! That was one for another day though.

Mostly, he thought about the old man. At one point, Sam wondered if he had dreamed the events of the last six hours or so. It just seemed so unreal that someone would take him, a street urchin, into their home and immediately trust him with the run of the place.

Getting up, he did a quick investigation of the flat before returning to the kitchen. Everything seemed normal; there was nothing to indicate Charlie posed any sort of threat to him. This was his only real concern – the old man seemed to trust Sam but could Sam trust him? Did he have an ulterior motive for his generosity?

He shrugged. All he could do was see how it played out. Going into the small living room, he switched on the television. Finding an old film that had just started, he stretched out on the sofa and settled down to watch it.

He was still on the sofa when Charlie returned, very

noisily, to the flat at 1.30 the following morning. In a deep sleep, Sam woke with a start, unaware of where he was for a second or two. Then he heard the toilet flush and remembered he was in the old man's flat. He heard Charlie come lurching out of the bathroom and across into the kitchen where he proceeded to clatter about noisily.

Getting up, Sam went to see what he was doing. A strong smell of alcohol hung in the air and he realised the old man was pissed. He shook his head disgustedly – he'd seen this so many times with his parents. However, unlike his mother who got nasty when drunk, Charlie just seemed to have lost control of his tongue. Busy doing something on the worktop, he was chuntering away happily to himself.

Turning to leave the kitchen with what looked vaguely like a cheese and tomato sandwich in his hand, much of its contents dripping onto the floor, Charlie suddenly saw Sam standing in the doorway and stopped dead with a look of astonishment on his face. It was obvious the old man had completely forgotten about him.

'Who the fuck are …?' he began in a slurred voice. Then recognition swept across his grizzled features. 'Sorry. You're up late lad, I'd have thought you'd be tucked up by now.'

'Fell asleep in front of the TV. Sorry if I startled you.' Sam yawned. 'I'll turn in now.' Stopping at the bedroom door, he looked back at Charlie. 'You haven't forgotten you're going to teach me how to pickpocket have you?' 'You're keen, aren't you? No, don't worry my boy, your lessons will begin tomorrow. I'm looking forward to it myself actually – it's time I retired. And before I do, it would be good to pass on what I know to someone like yourself who will find it useful.'

Sam eyed him uncertainly before nodding and going into the bedroom. If Charlie's sozzled state was anything to go by, he doubted that anything much would happen tomorrow. He had the feeling that the old man meant it though, so hopefully, if not tomorrow, it would happen another day.

The next morning, he was woken by the sound of loud cheerful singing. He'd slept in his clothes so didn't have to bother getting dressed. Opening the bedroom door, he could tell immediately that the singing was coming from the kitchen. Walking across to the entrance, he stood in bleary eyed surprise at the sight of the old man busily frying bacon, eggs, tomatoes and mushrooms, all the while singing his head off in accompaniment to the radio perched on top of the fridge. He was clearly in good fettle and apparently suffering no ill effects from his drinking of the previous night.

Turning to get something from the fridge, Charlie spotted him and beamed, 'There you are Sam. Breakfast will be ready in a few minutes.' The friendliness in his manner was unmistakeably genuine and, at that moment, Sam's last doubts about him disappeared.

As they sat eating their breakfast shortly afterwards, Sam studied the old man. He was clearly fresh and alert and, judging by the rate at which his breakfast was disappearing, in very good appetite. He couldn't believe this was the same man who had been so drunk just a few hours ago.

Charlie had fallen silent while he wolfed his food down but as soon as he was finished, he pushed his plate back and looked across at Sam. 'Right lad. I promised I would teach you the noble art of picking pockets and so I shall. Your first lesson starts now and is just talk, so listen up while you eat your breakfast.'

'I'm listening,' Sam mumbled through a mouthful of bacon.

Charlie lit a cigarette, took a deep drag, leant back in his chair and exhaled. 'Before I get into the mechanics of picking pockets, the very first thing you need to understand is that it's impossible for a person to think of more than one thing at a time. The human brain simply isn't capable of doing it. That basic fact is what makes it possible to pick someone's pocket. If the mark's attention is on something other than his money, he won't notice you taking it from him.'

As the old man talked, Sam noticed for the first time the nicotine stains on his fingers and how raspy his voice was. He was obviously a very heavy smoker.

'Now, before you even think of picking someone's pocket, you need to know where to do it and who to do it to. Get either of these wrong and you'll soon be in trouble. What you did yesterday is a good example of the right place to do it. You were out in the open so even though you were spotted, you were able to get away. Picking pockets in confined spaces, such as a bus or train, is much riskier because there's nowhere to go if you are seen. As for who you should target, ideally, it should always be someone you can fight off if necessary or outrun. No matter how good you are at the actual act of picking a pocket, there will be times when you get caught doing it. When that happens, you do not want to be facing someone bigger or stronger than yourself. With me so far?' Charlie blew out a cloud of smoke and looked keenly at the boy.

Sam swallowed the last of his breakfast before nodding, 'Makes sense.'

'Good. Now, unfortunately, this means the only people either of us should be targeting are older people. You because you're just a youngster and me because I'm getting to be an old git myself. I know it's not very nice but that's how it is. How do you feel about that?'

'I don't want to rob anyone, young or old, but I don't have much choice, do I?' Sam shrugged.

The old man nodded. 'Exactly. It's the same for me. We do what we have to to survive. You're much better placed than I am though – another five or six years and you'll be a strapping young man able to go after anything that moves. Whereas I ....' Charlie voice tailed off and he stubbed out the cigarette. There was a sadness on his face for a split second and then it was gone. Sam didn't miss it though and wondered.

'Observation is an essential part of picking pockets,' Charlie was swiftly back on track. 'You have to know where the money is – it's no good guessing. Sometimes, it's obvious. A wallet sticking out of a back pocket for example. But most people are sensible enough to keep it out of sight. So how do you find out where they've put it? Any ideas?'

Sam was paying close attention to the old man. He knew he was getting an invaluable lesson. 'Well, you say observation is essential so it must be about where to observe from.' He pondered the question for a few moments. 'I know,' he said suddenly, 'in a bank. You watch them withdraw their money and see where they put it. Yes?'

Charlie shook his head. 'No, the bank staff would soon be on to you. You're close though. A cash machine is much better. These things are all over the place – high streets, shopping centres, airports, etc. The important thing is that they're out in the open with people coming and going, which means, assuming you do it correctly, no-one will notice you. There's plenty of other places as well – bookies at race meetings and tourist attractions to name just two.'

'What about the police though?' Sam queried. 'Those are just the sort of places they'll be watching surely?'

The old man laughed derisively. 'There was a time when you'd have been right, but those days are long gone. Policemen on foot are few and far between now – they love their squad cars too much.' Charlie Parker clearly didn't have a high opinion of the British police force.

'So, having established where the mark has his money stashed, you then need to figure out the best way to get at it. If you're lucky it will be in an outside pocket or the top of an open bag, in which case straightforward sleight of hand will do the trick. However, if it's in an inside pocket or a closed bag, things are much more difficult.'

He paused to light another cigarette. 'The trick in this situation is to distract the mark. This is where people's inability to think of more than one thing at a time comes into play, and it requires two, or more, pickpockets operating as a team. A typical example of how it works is for one person to walk or stand right in front of the mark. Another then walks up from behind and falls against the mark as if by accident. This pushes the mark against the person in front and suddenly he finds himself in a situation where he has two people to deal with. Angry with the one who pushed him and thus distracted, it is now much easier to pick his pocket. With one in front and one behind, he simply cannot concentrate on both at the same time. Most professional pickpockets work in a team.'

'Have you ever worked in a team?' Sam asked curiously.

Charlie nodded. 'Yeah, but not for a while now. I prefer to work by myself these days. I don't make as much because I have to be more careful who I target, but it's safer.'

'Would you work with me?'

'I might. It all depends on whether you're good enough.'

'Would you trust me though?'

'Yes, I think I would.'

'How can you say that? We only met yesterday.' Sam was incredulous.

'I just do – that's all I can say. I trust my instincts and

they're telling me that you're sound. What are yours say-ing? Do you trust me?'

Sam considered the question. He had only known Charlie for literally a few hours but already he found him-self liking the man. He was friendly, generous and there was clearly an empathy between them, both seemingly having had much the same start to life. Somewhat to his surprise, he heard himself say quietly, 'Yes, I think I do.'

Pushing back his chair, Charlie Parker got to his feet. 'Fantastic. That's enough talking for now. Go and get yourself ready and then I'll take you out and give you a demonstration.'

He raised his open palm and, without hesitation, Sam high-fived him. At long last in his hitherto miserable life, things were looking up. He felt a surge of optimism the like of which he had never experienced before.

15 Years Later

Placing his drink on a corner table where he would have an unobstructed view of the saloon, Dave Collins sat down. Lighting a cigarette, he cast a disinterested look around. As might be expected on a Saturday evening, the Mitre was heaving with thirsty customers. None more so, it seemed, than a group of young women sitting at the table next to him. From the squeals of laughter, they were clearly intent on a good night out.

He was eyeing them appraisingly, when one, a particularly attractive redhead, caught him looking at her. With a half-smile, she held his eye for a moment before turning away. Any other time, he wouldn't have hesitated but he wasn't in the pub to pull; he was there on business. In any case, he had more important things on his mind.

Collins was a troubled man and had been for a while. His current line of work was exposing him to dangers that just weren't worth the risks. The business he was engaged on tonight was a typical example. It couldn't go on as it was. So, he had put his thinking cap on and come up with a plan. Potentially hugely rewarding if it worked, he would be set for life. If it didn't, he'd be banged up in prison. And that was the dilemma exercising him now – should he or shouldn't he! If he didn't, in all likelihood, he would end up back where he had started. And the prospect of that filled him with dismay.

Collins had been born into a fishing family in Folkestone down on the south coast. On leaving school at 16, he had gone straight into the family's fishing business. Unfortunately, he hadn't taken to it. He stuck it for seven years but then one morning woke up and realised he'd had enough. Word had it that London was where it was all at, and so it was that one chilly December morning, aged 23, he arrived at the capital's St Pancras railway station. Initially, as are many people new to London, he was simply bewildered by the commotion, the traffic, the crowds and what was to him the almost insane pace of life. It was as though he had been transported to a different world.

It was just what he was looking for however, and he quickly took to it. It was interesting, exciting and one never knew what was around the corner. He soon found a job working as a barman in a busy casino in Leicester Square called the Golden Horseshoe. The job itself was nothing special but the money was good and enabled him to rent a small flat and still have enough left over for getting out and about.

Another plus of the job was the women. The casino was full of them – wives, girlfriends, women on the make and hookers. As if they weren't enough, the casino itself employed a good number of women – croupiers, bar staff and waitresses. Everywhere Collins looked, in fact, he saw women and, as a red-blooded 23 year-old male, he took full advantage. It wasn't long before he scored with one of the casino's floor managers, an Irish lady called Ava. She was a lot older than him but still attractive, and she introduced him to a lot of interesting places and scenes.

All-in-all, his first year in London turned out to be well beyond his expectations. There was plenty of partying, he made a lot of friends, a few enemies, and developed some useful contacts. Then it all went wrong. It started when he lost his job at the casino due to turning up for work one evening still under the influence of a cannabis session earlier in the day. Suddenly back in the job market, he discovered that the only things on offer were menial and low paid. The first one he took involved serving pizzas in a fast food joint, but the money was so bad it barely covered his living expenses. With nothing left for socialising, he was forced to spend his time off stuck in the pokey flat watching the crap on the TV.

And so it went on. A succession of dead-end jobs over a period of six months or so that enabled him to survive, but only just. Eventually, in desperation, he turned to drug dealing. He had started smoking cannabis while working at the casino and had developed some contacts in the trade. One of these got him a job as a runner doing the donkey work of delivering the drugs to clients. It was well paid and solved his money issues literally overnight. However, it wasn't long before he discovered the downsides of being a runner. One was that he was the lowest of the low in the gang hierarchy. While the money was still good by most people's standards, it was little more than loose change in comparison to what those higher up in the chain were making. Another was that he was the one taking all the risks, not just of being caught by the police, but of being attacked by rival gangs. He knew of several runners who had been ambushed and robbed by rivals. Indeed, in a recent case, one of them had been beaten so badly, he'd ended up in hospital. Incredibly, on coming out, he was promptly stabbed to death by his own gang because he had lost the takings.

It was becoming an increasingly dangerous business to be in, abetted in no small part by the almost total lack of interest shown by the police. Indeed, it had reached the point now that Collins was apprehensive every time he went out to do a deal. He knew he had to get out of it soon before something bad happened to him. But, of course, that left the problem of how to make ends meet. Delivering pizzas and suchlike didn't pay enough; he needed something much better. Hence the plan.

A sudden cough shook him from his reverie. Looking up, he saw a tall, well-built man in his thirties staring down at him. Shaven headed, heavily tattooed and with a hard face, he was an intimidating sight. Sweating heavily, the fellow was clearly agitated about something.

'Are you Dave?'

Collins nodded.

'I'm Les.' It was the customer he had been waiting for. The man had identified him by the yellow baseball cap he was wearing.

Collins now noticed that he was shaking badly. That and the unnatural sweating were sure signs of drug withdrawal, and desperation for another fix. He'd seen this before and it always unnerved him because he knew people in this state were capable of anything.

'Okay, give me a few minutes and I'll meet you across the road,' he growled unhappily. He really didn't like the look of this one.

Five minutes later, he left the pub and headed across the street where he could see the man prowling restlessly up and down. As he went, he scanned the street in both directions to make sure they didn't have any unwelcome attention. When they were face-to-face, Collins held out his hand and demanded, 'The money first.'

It was as though the junkie could literally smell the skunk. Hopping from foot to foot, his hand shook almost uncontrollably as he held out some £20 notes.

Taking the cash, Collins counted it before handing over the package of skunk cannabis.

Slipping it into a pocket, the junkie turned to go then suddenly did an about turn and tried to snatch the money back. Half-expecting the move, Collins was ready for it and pushed him away.

With a cry of fury and pent-up frustration, the junkie punched him brutally in the face twice before running off down the street empty handed. Collins reeled back and fell to the ground.

That same Saturday evening, Sam Clark was also in the Mitre. It was one of his favourite pubs and he had been drinking there for a number of years. That wasn't the only reason he used it though. A lot of well-to-do people drank in the Mitre and he had found it a very lucrative place to do business. All he had to do was sit patiently and watch the idiots get pissed before relieving them of their cash.

This particular evening, however, his mind was on other things. He'd been picking pockets for fifteen of his twenty-five years and living with the constant risk of being arrested and jailed. It hadn't happened yet but he knew one day his luck would run out. If it had just been just him, it wouldn't have mattered so much but Sam now had a partner and a four year-old son. He wanted his boy to have a normal upbringing free of worry, unlike his own. The painful memory of his early years had never left him.

However, having been off the radar since he was ten, and with no employment record, there was no way he'd ever be able to get a proper job. His only option was to set up a business of some kind, and to do that he needed hard cash. Unfortunately, he didn't have enough. With the normal avenues of finance closed to him, he had to find another way of raising it.

He needed to pull off something big – something lucrative enough to set him up in one hit. The trouble was, what? Sam had pondered on this over and over again but had yet to come up with anything feasible.

Finishing his pint, he got to his feet and weaved through the throng to the bar. As he tried to catch a bartender's eye, there was a voice to his right. 'Hello darling. Are you looking for company?'

Turning, he saw a young woman in her twenties smiling at him. He knew immediately she was a hooker. The heavy makeup and suggestive manner were instant giveaways. From the sound of her, she was Eastern European, probably Rumanian. A lot of the whores in London were from that part of the world.

'Sorry love,' he smiled, 'I'll have to decline your kind invitation. Maybe another time.'

She gave him a look of mock disappointment before turning away with a suggestive wiggle of her hips. Sam watched her go admiringly; she had a great ass.

'Go on Sammy boy, you know you want to.'

Turning his eyes away from the woman's swaying rump, he turned to see Lucas, one of the Mitre's barmen, watching him amusedly.

'I doubt I could afford her,' Sam chuckled. He had a good relationship with the pub's bar staff, which came in handy when trying to get a drink at busy periods.

'You're getting old mate, that's your trouble,' Lucas shook his head sadly as he poured another pint of London Pride. 'On the slate?' As a regular customer, Sam had the privilege of being to settle his bar account monthly. He nodded.

'I could arrange to have her put on the slate as well if you like,' the barman persisted, grinning at his own wit.

Sam groaned. 'Oh, you're so funny. Why don't you fuck off and do something useful.' He liked Lucas; he was a cheerful character and always good for a laugh.

Going back to his seat, he decided to put his problems to one side for a while and just enjoy his pint. Gazing around, he saw the place was filling up rapidly. At the table next to him were five very happy Arsenal supporters celebrating their team's win earlier in the day. Beyond them, he could see an elderly couple engaged in a heated argument about something or other. He couldn't help but smile as he noticed the man seemed to be getting the worst of it – was it ever thus!

At a large table to his right sat a group of young women who were clearly out for a good time judging from the general merriment and risqué comments, not to mention the copious amount of alcohol that was flowing. He was listening with amusement to one of them describing a work colleague's recent pathetic attempt to chat her up, when he noticed a tall man come in.

Standing just inside the door, the man scanned the room, clearly looking for someone. There was an edgy, agitated look about him that Sam knew only too well. It may have been fifteen years ago but he could still remember his father looking exactly the same when in need of a fix.

Apparently spotting who he was looking for, the man started forward and passed right by Sam on his way to a table on the other side of the women. As he got close, Sam could see he was sweating heavily and was tattooed on his arms and neck. He didn't smell too good either.

Stopping at the table, the junkie stared down at its sole occupant – a short stocky man in his late- twenties wearing a yellow baseball cap. After a very brief exchange – they could have spoken barely a couple of sentences between them – the junkie turned and left the pub. Shortly afterwards, the other man got to his feet. He took a quick, surreptitious look around the crowded bar before heading to the door himself. He had a somewhat furtive manner about him, and Sam was pretty certain a drugs deal was about to take place. If so, hard cash would be changing hands and, ever the opportunist, he knew it could provide an opportunity to make some money.

Usually, he steered well clear of drug dealers. While a successful hit on one often resulted in a nice pay-out, they tended to be a violent breed and, from past experience, he knew they really weren't worth the risk. This one, however, didn't look particularly threatening. As he went past, Sam could see he was short and flabby. Nor did he exude the air of menace that many dealers did. Thinking this could be a nice earner with minimal risk, he got to his feet and followed him to the exit. Stopping outside the door, he saw the man cross to the far side of the street where the junkie was pacing up and down the pavement in a very agitated manner.

It was over in less than a minute. Sam watched the exchange take place and the junkie try to snatch his money back. Failing, he punched the dealer twice before running off.

As the dealer staggered back from the blows to his head and fell to the ground, Sam dashed across to where he lay. Although dazed, the man managed to slip the wad of notes into an inside jacket pocket. Sam didn't miss it. Kneeling down beside the semi-conscious man, he exclaimed in a voice full of concern, 'Are you all right?'

Dave Collins's head was spinning from the savage punches. He was only vaguely aware that someone was kneeling next to him and had said something.

'Can you hear me?'

Looking up, he saw a young man staring down at him. Touching his head gingerly, he mumbled confusedly, 'What the fuck happened?'

'Someone hit you mate. I was just coming out of the pub over there when I saw a guy punch you. You went down like a sack of potatoes.'

'Yeah, I remember now. He was trying to mug me,' Collins lied. He pulled himself into a sitting position. 'Help me up will you?'

'No problem.' Bending down, Sam slipped a hand under the man's left armpit and carefully hoisted him to his feet. At the same time, with a speed and dexterity born of years of practice, his other hand reached inside the dealer's jacket and came away with the wad of cash. Collins was completely unaware he had just been robbed.

'Can you walk?'

Taking a tentative step forward, the dealer staggered but managed to remain on his feet. 'Yeah, I think so.' His head was throbbing hard now and his mouth hurt like hell. 'Fuck, I feel like shit.'

'Do you want me to call an ambulance?'

'No, no.' Pulling out his phone, he said, 'I'll get a taxi to take me home.' He sounded very sorry for himself.

Looking at him, Sam could well understand why. There was a nasty looking lump coming up on his forehead and his lower lip was split and oozing blood. Sam couldn't help but feel sympathetic towards him. In fact, he was starting to feel a bit guilty for taking advantage of the man's plight by stealing his money. The least he could do was help him.

'Listen, I'm parked not far from here. How about I give you a lift to the nearest accident & emergency dept. From the look of you, I don't think it would be a bad idea.'

Wiping his hand across his lip, Collins looked at the blood. 'Yeah, you're probably right. It won't be putting you out too much?'

'Not at all mate. Wait here and I'll pick you up in a few minutes.'

Letting out a sigh, Collins shuffled over to a nearby lamp post and let it take his weight gratefully. He knew how lucky he had just been — it could as easily have been a knife. No more than half an hour ago he'd been thinking it was time to give up dealing; now there was absolutely no question about it. He'd come close before but this was the first time he'd actually been attacked. It had to be the last – the rewards from dealing in drugs were good but not that good!

Minutes later a car pulled up alongside. Leaning across, Sam opened the passenger door with a cheery, 'Come on then, we'll soon have you sorted out.'

Collins eased himself into the car gingerly. His head was clearing now and he wasn't sure he really needed medical attention but as he was getting a free lift, he may as well go.

'Okay?' Sam glanced at the dealer. The man just nodded. His lip was still bloody but apart from that he didn't seem too bad.

'Do you know where the nearest A&E is?' Sam asked. 'The only one I know of is over in South Norwood, near where I live.'

Collins nodded. 'There's one in Frith Street not far from here.' He glanced at his watch. 'At this time on a Saturday night though, it will be heaving with drunks.'

'Not to mention hooligans brawling in the streets.'

The dealer groaned. 'A comedian! That's all I need right now.'

Sam laughed. Entering a number on his phone, he said, 'I'll just give my partner a rang and let her know what's happening.' With that done, they set off.

They hadn't gone far before Collins said bitterly, 'Never a policeman around when you want one is there? That bastard could have killed me.'

Sam could hardly believe what he was hearing. The man had just been openly selling drugs on the street and now had the brass-neck to complain about the lack of police presence. Not too fond of drug dealers given his father's tragic life, it was only the fact the guy had just had a hell of a shock and was probably just letting off steam, that stopped him snapping a biting response.

Instead, he just said, 'So what's new? You can go weeks without seeing one where I live. Just as well too.'

Collins gave him a curious glance at this but said nothing.

They'd been driving in silence for about five minutes when he asked, 'What's your name?'

'I'm Sam. You?'

'Dave.'

Having introduced himself, Collins became more chatty and, for the rest of the journey prattled on, mainly about football and women. He was in the middle of a tale concerning two strippers called Sofia and Nikki he and a pal had taken out a few weeks ago, when they arrived at the A&E.

Turning to Collins, Sam said, 'Right, go in and get yourself sorted. I'll wait for you here and then drive you home.'

'No man, it's good of you to offer but I'll call a taxi. You get off home to your partner, it's already late.'

'Nah, you're all right. She already knows I'm going to be late. Besides, I want to hear what happened with the strippers.'

Collins laughed. 'Seriously, it could be a long wait. You

know what these places are like.'

'I shouldn't think so. There can't be too much wrong with you judging by the way you've been rabbiting on.'

'I do tend to go on, I know. All right then, I'll be as quick as I can.' Getting out of the car, he disappeared into the A&E building. Three-quarters of an hour later, he was back. His head was bandaged and his split lip had been stitched.

'Well, you certainly look a bit more human,' Sam commented as the dealer settled himself in the passenger seat. 'How are you feeling?'

'Much better thanks. The doctor said it's superficial and to just take it easy for a couple of days.'

'Good. Where to then?'

'Blackstock Road in Islington. Shouldn't take more than twenty minutes or so from here. Are you sure though? – I can get a taxi.'

'Absolutely.'

The streets were quieter now, and it wasn't long before they were motoring down Blackstock Road.

'Drop me off over there.' Collins pointed to a house coming up on the left. As Sam stopped the car, he said, 'Thanks man, I really appreciate what you've done for me tonight. Can we meet up sometime? I'd like to buy you a drink.'

'I'm in the Mitre most Saturday nights – why don't you pop in?'

Collins nodded. 'I'll do that. Thanks again.'

Twenty-five minutes later, Sam was inching the car into

the ridiculously tight space that was, according to the housing company's brochure, a spacious driveway. From the dim light showing through the curtains, he could see Katie had waited up for him. Curled up on the sofa reading a book, she looked up as he came in. 'What on earth have you been doing all this time?' she asked. There was a peevish note in her voice.

Throwing himself down next to her, he stretched out his legs and yawned wearily. 'Nothing really; just helping someone out. Get me a coffee and I'll tell you about it.'

'Here, have mine; I've only just made it.'

He nodded his thanks before relaying the events of the evening. When he'd finished, she asked with some surprise, 'Why on earth did you get involved with the man?'

'Because of what we've been talking about so much recently, I suppose. About me going straight. Tonight, for the first time in my life, I felt guilty about robbing someone. I felt sorry for the guy and so I helped him. And I'm glad I did.'

Leaning over, she gave him a big hug. Although Katie knew all about her partner's unfortunate upbringing and so understood why he had to steal, there was nothing she wanted more than for him to give it up. Ever since they'd set up home together, she had been expecting to see the police standing at the front door one day. At the same time, she was also worried. The hard fact was that they simply couldn't manage without the money he made from his crooked activities. The meagre salary she earned from her job as a cashier at the local bank just about covered the mortgage. Sam's money paid for everything else.

Yet another concern was their son. Sam's "self-employed" status meant he could pick and choose the hours he worked and so was able to look after the boy during the day while she was at work. If he had a proper job though, and had to work normal hours, who was going to look after him?

And as if all that wasn't enough, there was the fact that the authorities didn't know Sam even existed. This meant that everything had to be in her name – the mortgage, credit cards, bank accounts – everything! It just made things even more complicated than they already were.

'I can't do it anymore,' he continued. 'I don't know why but what happened tonight is a turning point for me. As of now, I'm finished with crime. I have to be for the lad's sake anyway. So far, he's been too young to be affected by the way we've been living but he's getting to the age now where he's going to be increasingly aware of things. Especially as he will be starting school in a few months. I'm not having him find out his dad is a common thief.'

The last sentence was spoken with some feeling and Katie reached over and squeezed his hand. There was an emotional edge to Sam's voice now, and she knew he was in deadly earnest.

'We've got about £4000 in cash. That will keep us going until I get something sorted.' He didn't sound entirely convinced of what he was saying though.

'Let's just take it one step at a time,' she said as reassuringly as she could. 'As you say, we have enough money for the time being. There's no immediate problem.'

He smiled at her affectionately. 'You're too good for

the likes of me.'

She laughed. 'I know. Have you only just realised?'

Sam chuckled. 'Time for bed I think.' Getting to his feet, a thought struck him. 'By the way, how's the old man? I haven't seen him since yesterday.'

Katie sighed. 'Not too good I'm afraid. He's been in his room all day. I had to take his dinner up to him again.'

'Did he eat any of it?'

She shook her head.

The old man was Charlie Parker – the kind-hearted old pickpocket who had befriended Sam all those years ago and rescued him from a life of destitution. Sam had lived with Charlie in his council flat for eleven years, and the old man had taught him all the tricks of his trade while providing him with everything he needed. In return, he'd asked for very little, letting Sam come and go as he pleased and interfering in his life as little as possible. He'd made no attempt to be a father figure.

It was perhaps inevitable though, that Sam came to see him as just that – the father he had never really had. Charlie had shared with him his knowledge of the world, taken him out and about to zoos, parks, fairs, restaurants – all experiences which had been completely foreign to him. He'd even taken the boy to a couple of holiday camps by the seaside. Sam had loved those.

The old man was by no means perfect, however. He was an irascible old devil at times and could fly off the handle at a moment's notice, particularly when he had been drinking. It never lasted long though. He was always soon back to his usual good-humoured self.

His main problem was his unhealthy lifestyle. He drank heavily, chain-smoked and did as little exercise as possible. It wasn't surprising really; from what little he had told Sam, he'd had a lonely life, having never married or had children. Alcohol, tobacco and food had been his only real pleasures.

Sam was eighteen and had been with Charlie for eight years when it began to catch up with him. It was gradual to begin with; shortness of breath, tiredness, lack of appetite – all symptoms of alcohol and tobacco poisoning.

Sam now found that, increasingly, he was looking after Charlie rather than the other way around. He "earned" most of the money and, as time went on, did more and more of the shopping, cooking, cleaning and the 101 other household chores. Given what the old man had done for him, he was more than happy to oblige.

However, when one day he found himself virtually carrying a wheezing Charlie up the stairs to the flat, he realised that something was going to have to change, and soon. And luckily it did.

One evening, shortly afterwards, Sam called in at a local pizza shop to get some dinner for the two of them. On this particular evening, Sam was served by a girl he hadn't seen in the place before. According to the label on her uniform, her name was Katie and he was taken with her immediately. However, not the most socially confident of people, he couldn't pluck up the courage to establish contact with her. Fortunately, she was equally taken with him and soon gave up waiting for him to make the first move. Opening his pizza box one evening, Sam found a scribbled note inside with her name and phone number.

The very next night, much to her amusement, he took her to an upmarket pizza restaurant in Mayfair. Sam had winced on seeing the bill, but when she kissed him at the end of the evening, he knew it had been money well spent.

Charlie had thought so as well, muttering, 'Perhaps we can stop having fucking pizzas every night now.'

Katie was new to London, have only recently come down from Milton Keynes. She was sharing a flat with an old school friend who she'd kept in touch with when she started dating Sam. Within a couple of months, they decided to set up home together. The baby soon followed, and everything was great apart from one thing – Charlie Parker! Even though he was no longer living with Charlie, Sam did everything he could to ensure the old man's wellbeing. He visited him at least once a week, phoned every night to check he was all right, and he and Katie had him round to eat with them regularly.

Nevertheless, once Sam had moved out, the old man went downhill rapidly. It wasn't even a year before Sam mooted the idea of him coming to live with them so he could be looked after properly. With a baby to see to, Katie wasn't at all keen on the idea. However, she recognised that Sam owed the old man a huge debt and simply had to do it.

It wasn't too bad to start with. No longer faced with flights of stairs to get in and out, Charlie was able to come and go as he pleased and spent a lot of time in the local bars with his pals. They didn't actually see that much of him. Then the emphysema took a deeper hold. Now, he was so short of breath it was all he could do to move from room to room. Around this time, he developed cirrhosis, caused by the years of heavy alcohol consumption. Combined, the two diseases left him in a permanent state of exhaustion, weakness and pain. His muscles quickly wasted away and within six months of moving into the house with them, he was virtually bed bound.

As they headed up the stairs that fateful evening, Sam had a feeling the old man wouldn't be a problem for much longer. He hadn't eaten a thing for two days now, so it was really just a question of time.

'Beer and a large whisky please Lucas.'

The barman nodded. 'Coming up. By the way Sam, everyone here was really sorry to hear about Charlie. He was a one-off.'

'Yeah, he was that.' Raising the whisky glass, Sam said, 'Here's to the old boy.'

Charlie had passed away just days after Sam's encounter with the drug dealer, Dave Collins, and was laid to rest a week later. For Sam, it was like losing a father and it had taken him quite a while to get over it.

Today though, he'd decided it was time to put the past where it belonged and move on with his life. So here he was in the Mitre, the pub that the old man had taken him out to for his first drink on turning eighteen. Sitting at the bar, Sam was idly flicking through his phone a while later when there was a voice behind him. 'Can I buy you that drink now?'

Looking round, he saw the stocky figure of Dave Collins standing there with a faint smile on his face.

'Hello there.' Sam was surprised. He hadn't been expecting to see the man again. 'Thanks, I'll have another whisky.'

'I'll get a bottle.'

Finding a table, they sat down.

'Well,' Sam said. 'You look a lot better than you did the last time I saw you.'

Collins nodded. 'Took me a few days to get over it, I can tell you.'

'I'm not surprised, you took a couple of nasty blows there.'

'Yeah, it wasn't a good night. Lost my phone as well. And some cash.' He sounded rueful.

'Ah, maybe not.' Pulling out his wallet, Sam took out some £20 notes and handed them to Collins. 'There's the £120 you lost.'

The man furrowed his brow as he stared at the money in his hand. 'I don't understand.'

'Think back. When were you last aware of having the cash?'

'When I put it in my pocket after falling down, I think! – it's a bit of a blur.'

'And what happened after that?'

'You helped me up.' It took a few moments but then the penny dropped. 'Of course, you must have taken it then.'

'It was like taking sweets from a baby,' Sam chuckled.

Collins shook his head in amazement. 'You're a pick-pocket! Well, I'll be damned.'

'Does that bother you?'

'No. Should it? It's no worse than what I do.'

Sam nodded. 'Yeah, I know what you do. You're a drug dealer.'

'What makes you think that?'

'I saw the whole thing that night. The guy who met you inside the pub was obviously a junkie and when you followed him outside, it was pretty clear what was going on. I saw a chance to make a hit so I followed you out. The guy then attacked you and, like the good Samaritan I am, I came over and helped you up. At the same time, I helped myself to your cash.'

Collins nodded slowly. 'I see.' A puzzled look crossed his face. 'But why did you help me afterwards by taking me to the A&E and then home. If it was just business for you, why did you bother? I wouldn't have.'

Sam was silent for a while as he considered how best to answer. In truth, it was a difficult one. It wasn't as clear-cut as just saying, 'I felt sorry for you.' His decision to help the man had been influenced by a number of factors, none of which were easy to explain to a virtual stranger. Would he even be interested?

'Guilt I suppose,' he said finally.

Collins shook his head. 'Sorry, you've lost me.'

'When I robbed you that night, for the first time in my life I felt guilt. I felt ashamed of what I'd just done.'

Sam could see from the blank expression on his companion's face that he wasn't following. 'You won't understand unless I tell you a bit about myself.' Lighting a cigarette, he continued, 'My parents were drug addicts. My dad died from an overdose when I was ten and my mother walked out on me just after. I was living on the streets when I had the good fortune to meet a wonderful old man who took me in. His name was Charlie and he was a pickpocket – a bloody good one. Charlie taught me everything there is to know about picking pockets and I've been doing it ever since. It's the only thing I know how to do.'

He could see Collins was listening with interest. 'What I'm trying to tell you is that I'm not a thief by choice; there was simply no other option for me.'

'Fucking hell, a thief with a conscience. I've heard it all now.' Collins shook his head. 'Well, if you're going to just hand it back, there's no point taking the risk of stealing it in the first place. So, you're just going to have to get yourself a proper job, aren't you?'

'If I could get a proper job, I'd have done it years ago. But, because I'm out of the system it's virtually impossible. All I'll get is cash-in-hand crap.'

Collins nodded. 'Yeah, I know where you're coming from there.' Reaching out for the bottle, he topped up their glasses. 'It's none of my business, but if you're not going to thieve anymore, and you can't get a proper job, what *are* you going to do?'

'That's the million-dollar question. Especially as I have a partner and a four year old kid to provide for. The only thing I can think of is to set myself up in a legitimate business of some sort and put it in my partner's name. Trouble is, it takes money to set up a business and I don't have enough,' Sam sighed gloomily.

'Hmm,' Collins said thoughtfully. 'This is interesting.

It could just be that we may be able to help each other out here.'

'How do you mean?'

'Well, as it happens, I'm in much the same situation as you are. I didn't set out to be a dealer. Circumstances forced me into it just as they forced you into picking pockets. I don't do too badly out of it, I will admit, but it's a fucking dangerous game to be in as you saw that night. And it's getting worse all the time. There's some right headcases out there, so I'm looking to get out before some fucker sticks a knife in me.'

He shook his head wonderingly. 'This seems a hell of a coincidence but it looks like I decided to stop dealing and you to stop thieving at about the same time. Has fate thrown us together do you think?'

'Are you offering to finance me then?' Sam smiled.

'Christ, you should be so lucky. I'm not exactly broke but I certainly don't have money to throw about.'

'Well, I'm in the same position. So how can we help each other?'

Collins leaned forward. 'Listen. You say you want to set up a business of some kind and need money to do it with. Well, I can't help you with the business. To be honest I'm not really interested in that. However, I do have a plan that can get us both a lot of cash and very quickly. In fact, if it works out, it will make us both rich – you won't even need a business. You'll be able to retire to a Caribbean island and spend the rest of your days lazing in the sun.'

'Sounds great,' Sam said sceptically. 'Why do you need

me though?'

'I can't do it by myself, simple as that really.'

'It's a stupid question I know, but does it involve anything illegal?'

'Well, how many things can you think of that make you rich quickly without breaking some law or other?' Collins said sarcastically.

'What is this plan then? How do I come into it?'

Collins was silent for a moment as though debating with himself. 'Before I tell you, let's get one thing straight. This is between us, understand?' There was a hard glint in the man's eye now and Sam didn't miss it. He nodded.

'Did you hear that story last week about six illegal immigrants drowning when their boat capsized in the Channel?'

'Yeah, it was in the newspapers.'

'That's the plan.'

Sam raised his eyebrows. 'Drowning illegal immigrants? How's that going to send me to the Caribbean?'

'No, you prat. Bringing them in – that's the plan. These people will pay anything up to ten grand for a ride across the Channel. It's money for nothing.'

Under normal circumstances, Sam would have made his excuses then and there and got out of the place. Unfortunately, due to his situation, things weren't normal and so he didn't. Instead, he looked at Collins and exclaimed, 'Are you serious?'

'Absolutely. What's to stop us?'

'What's to stop us?' Sam stared at him in amazement. 'Well, for one thing, there's the little matter of a suitable boat, not to mention the knowledge of how to use it. For another, how do we make contact with these immigrants? Then there's the Border Force people – they're not going to just wave us through. Give me a couple of minutes and I'm sure I'll be able to come up with a few more reasons.'

Collins raised his hands placatingly. 'I'm not saying it's going to be plain sailing, if you'll pardon the pun. As you correctly point out, there are quite a few issues that'll need to be sorted. All I'm saying at the moment is that it can be done. There's no doubt in my mind about it. What I want to know from you is, are you interested?'

Sam leaned back in his chair and ran a hand through his hair. 'Bloody hell. I'm still not certain this isn't a wind up.' He scrutinised Collins closely before saying carefully. 'I know there's a lot of this going on and clearly there's big money to be made from it. So, it is tempting. Plus, I need to do something soon. Not to put too fine a point on it, I'm getting desperate. So, if you can convince me it's feasible, yes, I might be interested.'

'Well, that's a start at least.' Collins stood up. 'Excuse me a moment while I go to the Gents.'

While he was gone, Sam took the opportunity to mull over what he'd said. The scheme was potentially very dangerous and he could scarcely believe he was even considering it. Still, he reasoned to himself, there nothing to be lost by hearing what Collins had to say. It was going to have to be bloody good though.

'Okay,' he said when Collins returned. 'Convince me.'

'Right then. Let's start with the two main things we're

going to need. The first is a load of immigrants and the second is a boat to ship them across in. Now with regard to the former, we're also going to need a contact in France to act as a go-between and organise things that end. That shouldn't be difficult – one of us will have to go across there and find one. I speak a bit of French so that'll be my job.'

'How come you speak French?' Sam asked in surprise.

'I had a French girlfriend for a couple of years. And she taught me a lot more than just French I can tell you,' Collins leered. 'Anyway, our second main requirement is a boat. Now, it just so happens that I come from a town called Folkestone. Do you know where it is?'

'Down on the south coast I think.'

'Yes. And almost directly opposite Folkestone, on the other side of the channel, is a place called Calais. Do you know what's in Calais?'

'French people?'

Collins rolled his eyes impatiently. 'Yes, but we're not interested in them. We're interested in illegal immigrants and Calais is where we'll find them – hundreds of them.'

Sam nodded, 'Yes, I remember reading about that now you mention it. These immigrants live in makeshift camps around Calais, don't they? Apparently, the French police give them a hard time.'

'That's right. Now listen to this. Before I came to London, I was a fisherman in Folkestone. My family have been fishing there for nearly two hundred years. I left school when I was sixteen and went straight onto the trawlers. I spent the best part of six years fishing in the

English Channel and I can tell you there's not much about that part of the world I don't know.'

From being deeply sceptical, Sam was suddenly taking a lot more interest in what he was hearing. 'Is that a fact? So, you're telling me if we can get hold of a suitable boat, you know how to handle it and get us to Calais and back again.'

'No problem at all. I can do it in my sleep.'

'And the boat?'

'Between them, my lot own three boats. We just need to borrow one of them. Either that or steal one from somewhere.'

'And what about the French and UK border forces? How do we avoid them?'

'Well, if you believe the politicians, there are fleets of border force vessels out there sweeping the Channel to prevent the immigrants getting in. It's the same story with the French. The reality, however, is totally different. Between them, they can only muster five or six, and half of those are usually laid up for one reason or another. On any one night, there may actually be only two or three vessels from both sides in action. So the chances of being caught by one of them is remote to say the least. Just to be absolutely sure though, we'll cross the channel in a section they don't patrol. Remember, they don't have enough boats to cover all of it. Also, most of the smuggling gangs don't have boats – they make do with dinghies powered by outboard engines. These have a limited range which means they have to take the most direct route across the channel. So the border forces only need to patrol a relatively small area as they know where the boats are likely to be. We, on the other hand, will be in a proper seagoing vessel that has a much larger range. This will enable us to sail right around the area patrolled by the border forces.'

Sitting back, Collins finished by saying, 'And that's it in a nutshell. As I hope you can see, the main elements are already taken care of. All that's needed is to sort out the minor details.'

Sam stared down into his glass thoughtfully. He was beginning to think the hare-brained scheme might actually have a chance of succeeding. After a long pause, he nodded, 'Yeah, I think it might be worth a try.' He couldn't help but feel a touch of apprehension as he said it though. This was something completely out of his league.

'Good.' Collins looked at his watch. 'I think that's enough for now.' He scribbled something on a beermat and pushed it across. 'Here's my number. If you want to ask me anything, just give me a call. Assuming you don't change your mind in the meantime, I suggest we meet at my place on Wednesday night about 8.00. We can go into it in more detail then. Agreed?'

'Yeah, that sounds good.'

'Great.' Collins got to his feet. 'By the way, I want you to keep this.' He tossed the wad of cash Sam had given him earlier on the table. 'You deserve it; it was a brilliant bit of thieving. I didn't notice a thing.'

Sam watched him leave and then, with a shrug, pocketed the money and headed for the exit himself. Stepping outside, he shivered in the cold night air. A light rain was falling and he swore, knowing he was going to have to walk home. The police were having one of their periodic crackdowns on drink-driving and it wasn't worth the risk. He'd have to leave his car in the side street where he'd parked it earlier and just pray it would still be there come morning. He shook his head disgustedly – you could always rely on the police being there for minor motoring transgressions, but they were never anywhere to be seen when cars were being vandalised or stolen.

As he made his way back, Sam mind was a jumble of conflicting thoughts. On the one hand, he couldn't believe he was even considering getting involved in the crazy scheme, especially as he knew virtually nothing about Collins. On the other, he knew he had to do something about his situation, and soon. It could be that the time had come to take a chance. Speculate to accumulate as the saying went.

By the time he arrived home, the only thing he was really sure about was that, thanks to the whisky, he was going to have a sore head the following morning. As to what Katie would make of it, well …!

With a three-inch screw done up tightly though each hand, the naked body was literally screwed to the door. It hung there motionless, knees buckled slightly and the feet dragging. Its midriff was sliced open and the entrails had been ripped out and hung down to the bloodied floor in a horribly gory mess. The victim had sustained other injuries as well. His face was battered brutally – a knuckleduster by the look of it, both elbows had been smashed and there were numerous cuts and bruises. Whoever the man had been, he had suffered a slow and agonising death.

Hayes studied the scene carefully, taking in every detail. Nine years in the police had taught him that there was little some human beings weren't capable of. Of all the terrible things he had seen, this was probably the worst though. Cynical and battle-hardened as he was, he couldn't help but shake his head in genuine sorrow as he imagined the suffering the poor creature must have gone through.

'Jesus Christ, what sort of animal could do a thing like

this,' Constable Steven Wiltshire whispered in horror. He had come in after Hayes and, on spotting the grisly remains of the victim, had immediately thrown up his lunch. In only his second year as a policeman, he had never seen anything remotely like it.

Hayes took him by the shoulder and turned him away gently from the gruesome sight. 'Don't look at it. Have a scout about and see if you can find something that might shed some light on this. I'll deal with the body.'

They were standing in a garage located in a quiet suburban street in Northwest London. The owner had gone out that morning to hang some washing in the back garden. She had been pegging a sheet on the line when she noticed blood oozing out from the bottom of the garage's rear door. Luckily for her, she had had the good sense to call the police rather than investigate it herself.

Hayes turned back to continue his inspection. On the wall alongside the door, a message had been written in dripping blood. It read: 'I fuck with us bros. We will cut yo fuckin harts out and feed yo to the fishes.'

He sighed. He had seen messages like this before. Invariably, they were menacing, illiterate and written in street language. They always indicated the same thing — turf wars. He knew there was very little likelihood that he and his colleagues would be able to apprehend the perpetrators of the dreadful crime. The gangs rarely, if ever, left anything that could be used as evidence.

He turned away to where Wiltshire was poking around in some cardboard boxes in the far corner. Deathly pale, the constable still looked queasy and was clearly wishing himself somewhere far away.

'Anything?' Even as Hayes spoke, he knew what the answer would be. Wiltshire looked around at him and just shook his head.

Hayes nodded. 'Okay, I've seen all I need to. The forensics team are on their way down. I want you to wait outside for them and make sure nobody else gets in here. I'll head back to the station and make out the report.'

Leaving the constable standing guard outside the garage, he got in his car and started the drive back to Bishopsgate Police Station where he was based. The investigation would almost certainly be a waste of time, he knew. Even if by some miracle they caught whoever had done it, the courts would hand down what passed for a life sentence these days of twenty years or so. With remission for good behaviour, the killer, or killers, would be back on the streets within as little as nine or ten years and then quite probably carry on just as before.

The pointlessness of it all didn't really bother him anymore. All he could do was catch the bastards; what happened after that was out of his control. It had made him cynical though. Cynical to the degree that he had soon figured he may as well do as so many of his colleagues were doing. Which was either keeping their heads down for a quiet life, or "making a bit on the side".

Hayes had opted for the latter option. While he was an excellent detective and always did his utmost to put a villain away wherever possible, money had become his main motivation. There were various ways a man in his position could do it: one of the main ones being "losing" incriminating evidence. Hayes had been paid a small fortune over the years to ensure that incriminating evidence against certain individuals disappeared inexplicably.

It took him nearly an hour to reach Bishopsgate where he shared a small office on the 2nd floor with Detective Inspector Ruby Williams. Looking up as he went in, she knew immediately from the expression on his face that he was upset.

'Bad one?'

Slumping down opposite her, he grimaced. 'Bad as I've ever seen. Here, have a look for yourself.' Taking out his phone, he slid it across to her.

Hayes watched her face pale as she scrolled through the pictures he had taken of the bloodied corpse in the garage. 'Oh my God! Was Steven with you?'

He nodded. 'Poor chap. He threw up.'

'I'm not surprised. I'm close to throwing up myself. Ugh.' She pushed the phone back. 'Any clues?'

'Nothing obvious. We'll have to wait and see if Forensics come up with anything. I'm not holding my breath though. These bastards know how to cover their tracks.' Switching his PC on, he logged in and started compiling his report.

Hayes clearly wasn't in the mood for chitchat, so she wisely shut up and left him to get on with it. Try as he might though, he simply couldn't get the awful image out of his mind. After a few minutes, he shoved the PC back with an exasperated, 'Fuck it, I can't do this now.' He wouldn't be able to do anything until he had cleared his mind, he knew. 'I'm going to the gym, back in an hour or so.'

'All right, I'll keep an eye on things here.' She was aware this was Hayes's way of de-stressing.

'Thanks Ruby.' He stopped at the door and looked back at her appreciatively. 'I'll have to take you out one night. You do a lot for me.'

She smiled at him. 'I'll hold you to that.'

Three-quarters of an hour later, Hayes was easing the 250-pound barbell back onto the rest with a grunt of relief. His triceps felt as though they were on fire and he lay there on the bench for a few moments letting them recover. He was just sitting up when a woman walked past and glanced at him with a smile. Clad in a tight-fitting leotard, he couldn't help but notice she had a fabulous figure.

Rubbing his upper arm, he looked up at her with a rueful grin. 'I sometimes wonder if it's worth it.'

She stopped. 'Definitely. You look good.'

'Thanks. You look in good shape yourself.' Blonde, well stacked and clearly fit, she ticked all Hayes's boxes. 'I haven't seen you in here before.'

'This is my first time. I haven't been in the area long and I'm still finding my way around. Do you come in here a lot?'

'At least three time a week; sometime more.'

The woman eyed his muscled torso. 'It shows.'

Hayes could see she was interested. 'Why don't you let me show you around?

The woman looked at him for a moment as though thinking about it and then nodded slowly. 'Yes, I might take you up on that.'

'Great.' Hayes got to his feet. 'I'm Jack.'

'And I'm Polly. Nice to meet you.'

'How about we start off with dinner in a nice Chinese restaurant I know. The food's excellent.'

'Sounds good. I love Chinese food.'

'Will tomorrow evening be all right?'

She laughed. 'You don't waste any time, do you? Yeah, go on then, why not.'

'I'll pick you up at 7.30.'

'I'll look forward to it. I live at 205 Penywern Road in Earls Court.'

Leaving the gym fifteen minutes later, Hayes was feeling much happier.

'This is the plan then. On Friday evening, I'll drive us down to a place called St Margaret's Bay. It's a remote place well off the beaten track and will be ideal. The car will be fitted with false number plates so we can't be traced from it. My brother, Ron, will be waiting for us with the fully fuelled boat. He's asked for £5000, which I think is fair. You happy with that?'

Sam nodded. 'Yeah, that sounds reasonable. How big is the boat?'

'Seven metres in length, three metres in width. It's a small one as fishing boats go but is perfect for our purposes. We'll be able to get at least twenty-five immigrants on board. At £10000 per head, that will be £250,000 for us. Minus expenses of course.' Dave Collins grinned, rubbing his hands together enthusiastically, before continuing. 'Ron will also see to it that the boat has a false identification number just in case we are seen at some point.'

'Don't boats these days have some kind of electronic identification system as well,' Sam queried.

'They do indeed. It's called AIS, which is short for Automatic Identification System. However, it's only mandatory on vessels that are sixteen metres or more in length. It's not something we need to be concerned about.'

'Okay.' Sam was determined to go through it step-by-step. 'We're on the boat. What then?'

Collins waved his phone. 'I contact our man in Calais and tell him our ETA. He'll be expecting it and will have the immigrants standing by. When he hears from me, he'll load them into a lorry and drive them to the rendez-vous point.'

'And where's that?'

'A place called Gironde Beach, which is a thirty-minute drive along the coast west of Calais. It's an isolated spot where no-one will see us. It'll take about an hour and a half to get there so the immigrants will be waiting when we arrive. Before we load them onboard, we take pay-ment.'

'How do we find our way to this beach?'

'That's probably the easiest bit. We use a GPS chart plotter.'

Sam looked blank. 'What's one of those?'

'Well, think of it as a car satnav but for boats. It's a device that has a screen of about twelve inches, which displays a map and your position on the map. It gets the position by using the Global Positioning System. Just as with a car satnav, you just tell it where you want to go and it directs you there. It's accurate to about ten metres,' Collins explained patiently.

'What about other vessels? How do we avoid running

into something?'

Collins smiled at Sam's naivety. 'The boat is fitted with radar, which is linked to the chart plotter and so automatically guides us around any obstacles and then gets us back on the correct course. It's virtually fool proof.' Tapping an eye, he added, 'plus of course, we use these.'

'Sounds good so far.'

'Right, when we arrive, we won't be able to beach the boat – it's too big. So, we'll have to anchor fifty metres or so offshore and then ferry the immigrants across. We'll do that with an inflatable dinghy that's towed behind the boat.'

There was a hint of amusement in Collins's eyes as he saw the pensive expression on his companion's face. 'Don't worry, I've thought it all through.'

Sam was unmoved. 'You're still going to have to explain it all to me. I'm not committing myself to this until I'm clear on every single detail.'

'That's fine; I don't expect you to.'

'As long as that's understood. Now then, what about payment? Are we talking cash, electronic transfer or what?'

Collins chuckled. 'Are you serious? It has to be cash. The immigrants will have already paid our contact. His fee will be fifteen percent, so he'll simply hand over the remaining eighty-five percent to us. Then we load them onboard and get on our way.'

Sam did some quick maths. 'That's a bit steep isn't it? Assuming we get £250,000, he'll be taking about £37,000 of it.'

'I know. He's not doing us any favours and that's a fact.' Collins shrugged. 'However, we don't really have a choice. He's the man on the ground. He knows the lay of the land over there and will organise the whole thing. That means we spend the minimum amount of time hanging around, which cuts the risk of getting caught considerably. All we have to do is take the money, load them aboard and sail back. Using him simplifies things enormously.'

'Yeah, I suppose so. What do we know about the guy though? Can we trust him?'

'Well, what do you think? I've only met him once when I went over to Calais last week. Would you trust a complete stranger?' There was a sombre look on Collins face as he continued, 'All I can say from our meeting is that he seems straightforward enough. In any case, I see no reason why he would renege on the deal. As far as he's concerned, we have a boat and he has what appears to be a limitless amount of these immigrants all desperate to get across the channel. He needs us as much as we need him. Particularly as I've told him we'll be back for more. Also, while I was out there, I took the opportunity to speak with some of the immigrants in the camp with regard to him. They confirm he is what he says he is.' Collins shook his head, 'No, I don't anticipate any problems there.'

'Who is he though? Where did you find him?' Sam was curious.

'I just know him as Michel. He's a local Frenchman who is obviously taking advantage of the situation over there. And who can blame him? He actually approached me when he heard that I was asking around. He told me he's by no means the only "organizer" there. Apparently, there's so much money to be made, the Eastern European gangs are beginning to move in. And they, my friend, are people you do not want to get involved with. They'll cut your throat as soon as look at you.'

'Hmm.' Sam was unsure but he let it go. He knew they wouldn't be able to eliminate every risk. 'What do we do if we are intercepted by either the French or UK Border Forces?'

'As I told you in the pub the other night, that's extremely unlikely to happen,' Collins said confidently. 'However, if it does, we simply do a runner.'

Sam frowned. 'What do you mean, do a runner?'

Collins laughed. 'Remember I said we'll be towing an inflatable dinghy? Well, it has a 300-horsepower outboard engine that will easily out-pace any coastguard vessel. At the first sign of trouble, we just jump on and speed off into the night. We'll be out of sight almost before they know we're there. In any case, they would be duty-bound to stop and rescue the immigrants. What happens to them then depends on whether it's the French or British Border Force.'

Sam nodded. 'Yes, I've heard that a lot of these people smugglers just abandon the poor sods in the middle of the sea. I don't want to be involved in anything like that.'

'Don't worry, neither do I. As I said, it'll only happen if we are intercepted, in which case the Border Force will take care of them.'

'Where do we land the immigrants when we get to the UK?'

'Back at St Margaret's Bay. Just as with Gironde Beach, it's a remote spot where we won't be seen. Once we've landed them, they're on their own. Ron will take care of the boat and we'll get out of there fast. Now, assuming it all goes to plan, I intend doing another four or five runs afterwards and then calling it a day before it gets too dangerous or our luck runs out.'

'Let's not get ahead of ourselves,' Sam cautioned. 'If I do this, it'll be on the basis of just one run initially. What happens after that depends on how it goes.' Turning his head, he stared out the window. It was mid-afternoon on an unseasonably warm and sunny April day and, outside, people were walking around in shorts and t-shirts. Holed up in Dave Collins living room, for a moment he wished he was out there with them rather than contemplating what he knew was an extremely risky venture.

Watching him keenly from across the table, Collins could see Clark still had reservations. He had put forward a reasoned, detailed and plausible plan but he had a feeling the man wasn't going to go for it. Knowing he couldn't pull the operation off by himself, he had to somehow persuade him to come aboard. What better to persuade him with than money!

He cleared his throat. 'Listen Sam. I can see you're not sure. Obviously, there are risks – a number of things could go wrong in fact. But that's life isn't it? – it's all a gamble. I'm quite happy in my own mind that we have a ninety-five percent chance of pulling this off. And re-member, if we do, we'll both be better off to the tune of £120,000 or so. Even if you then decide not to do any more runs, that should easily be enough to set you up in something legitimate. He who dares wins, yes?'

Sam was silent for a while before letting out his breath, 'What the fuck, let's go for it.'

A big grin split Collin's face and he let out a loud whoop. 'Attaboy. You know it makes sense.'

'How long before we're ready to go then?'

Collins thought aloud. 'Let's see. First, we contact Michel to let him know the operation is on. He told me he can have the immigrants ready to go within twenty-four hours. Then we contact my brother Ron so he can get the boat and inflatable dinghy organised. He'll need a couple of days for that. Assuming the weather is favour-able, I see no reason why we can't do it later this week.'

'As soon as that!' Sam raised his eyebrows in surprise.

'Absolutely. There's no reason not to.' Opening a drawer, Collins took out a phone. 'This is a burner phone – it's totally anonymous so there'll be no records of any calls or texts made with it. I'm going to contact Michel now and get the ball rolling.' Tapping the keys, he sent a text that read: 'We want to visit you this week.' The an-swer came back within a minute. 'Good. Let me know when to expect you.'

He grunted in satisfaction. 'Now I'll get hold of my brother. He sent the same message again and, as before, it wasn't long before confirmation arrived. Leaning back in his chair, Collins fixed Sam with a hard stare. 'Right then, it's in motion. All we have to do now is keep an eye on the weather. I've already had a look at the forecast and conditions in the Channel should be ideal for our purpose on Friday. So, assuming it doesn't change, I vote we do it Friday night. That okay with you?'

Sam was committed now. He nodded.

'Friday night it is then. Meet me here at 5.00pm.'

Standing, they shook hands and Collins walked him to the door.

As he drove home, he was dreading telling Katie what he had just agreed to. He'd told her about Collins and his plan several days ago and her reaction had been to forbid him to have anything to do with the man. She'd finished by telling him he was a complete idiot for even considering it.

Dave Collins waited until Sam had driven off before picking up his phone again. This time he made a call. 'We're on for Friday night. Be ready.' With that he hung up. In contrast to his earlier, almost wheedling manner with Sam, he was now abrupt and business-like.

Almost a different man, in fact.

Jack Hayes watched admiringly as Polly Santana strolled back to the table from a visit to the Ladies. Sitting down, her eyes fixed him with a look that he couldn't mistake. It was game on. He always tried to bed them the first night and, if he couldn't, he dumped them immediately. Hayes didn't believe in wasting time. There was no shortage of available women out there and he was well aware that he was just the type of man they were looking for – fit, good looking and with money in his pocket.

It was 10.00pm on a Saturday evening and they were sitting at a table in the popular Chojo Chinese restaurant in Westminster. It was expensive but what the hell, he could afford it thanks to his "sidelines". The food was delicious and also extremely healthy; something that was important to a keep-fit fanatic like Hayes. Just as importantly, it never failed to impress the women he took there. He knew that an expensive night out with good food, fine wine and plenty of old-world charm, when provided by a man with his good looks and seeming wealth, was something very few of them could resist.

They were invariably ready for it come the end of the evening.

Picking up the bottle of Chateau Chevalier de Larquey, he topped up their glasses. At £80 a time it was a lot more expensive than the stuff he usually bought but he had figured this one would be worth it.

He raised his glass. 'Cheers, I've really enjoyed this evening. I hope you have too.' He was lying though. Totally focussed on his career, making money and shagging as many women as he could, Jack Hayes was as narcissistic as they came. Capable of enormous charm when it suited him, he could switch to being cold and disinterested in an instant. When it came down to it, he was really only interested in women for the one thing. Most of them bored him rigid with their inane chatter. The one he was with now was a typical example. For a good two hours, he'd had to pretend to be interested in her life story, her hopes for the future, blah, blah, blah. The only thing she'd said that remotely interested him was that she'd just started a course training to be a fitness instructor. With a twinkle in her eye, she'd suggested she wouldn't mind practising on him. He'd laughed and said he was available any time.

Polly leaned forward and clinked her glass against his. 'I've enjoyed it as well. The dinner, the wine, you... Everything has been just perfect. Now I want you to take me back to your place and fuck me.' She looked deep into his eyes as she said it.

A rush of excitement swept through him. Most men would have been taken aback at her forwardness. Not

Jack Hayes. It wasn't the first time a woman had asked him outright like this.

He grinned. 'Ask and you shall receive.' Looking round, he waved the nearest waiter across and requested the bill. Service in a classy joint like the Chojo was top-notch and minutes later it arrived. Producing a wallet bulging with notes, Hayes paid in cash. 'Would you call me a taxi please Chen,' he asked the waiter.

'Certainly Mr Hayes.' Chen gave Polly a knowing glance. He had seen Hayes at it many times before and always it was with a different woman. As usual, this one was young and attractive.

'Thank you.' Hayes tipped the man a £20 note. Pulling his phone from a trouser pocket, he turned back to Polly. 'Excuse me a few moments while I check my messages. One of the downsides of being a policeman, I'm afraid – I have to keep on top of everything that's going on.'

She smiled. 'Don't take too long.'

Hayes had no idea he was dealing with someone every inch the sexual predator he was. Polly watched him as he sat there, flicking through his emails and texts. She'd re-alized two things almost immediately on meeting him at the gym. The first was that he was a womanizer, and the second was that he had a very high opinion of himself. It didn't matter though. From the look of him, he could satisfy her and that was all she wanted. Unless he was something exceptional in the bedroom department, which he probably wasn't – the ones who fancied them-selves were rarely as good as they thought they were – she'd quickly move on to the next one.

That was how she'd been thinking at the start of the evening. Anticipating a somewhat boring prelude to the lovemaking session that was to come, Polly had been pleasantly surprised to find her date was actually quite an interesting character. While much of what he said was related to his work as a policeman, and he had a tendency to overdo the macho stuff, some of the stories he told were quite fascinating. She couldn't help but compare Hayes with her last date – an extremely well-built builder who'd talked about nothing but football and drank pint after pint of lager. When the time for action had come, he hadn't even been able to get it up!

Suddenly impatient, she reached across the table and took the phone from him. 'Come on Jack, we're wasting good fucking time.'

She'd no sooner said it than Chen opportunely appeared at Hayes's elbow. 'Your taxi has arrived sir.'

Hayes grinned at her. 'Let's get to it then.'

They couldn't have picked a better night for it. The moon was hidden behind the clouds, there was a slight breeze and the sea was much calmer than Sam had expected it to be. Having never set foot on a boat in his life, he had been apprehensive about getting seasick but, as it turned out, he needn't have worried. Not only did he feel fine, he was actually enjoying the experience.

'We're about halfway across now.' As he spoke, Collins pointed out their position on the chart plotter; the instrument's LED screen casting a faint greenish glow in the cramped wheelhouse. 'Three quarters of an hour and we'll be there.' He glanced at his watch. 'Time to contact our French friend.'

Standing next to him, Sam watched as he tapped 'eta 1.30' on his phone and then hit the send key. Acknowledgement came back within seconds. Nodding in satisfaction, Collins went back to scanning the sea ahead of them.

Sam, meantime, was astonished at the amount of traffic in the Channel. As it was the early hours of the morning, he had expected they would have the seaway virtually to themselves. Instead, they were literally surrounded by other vessels, their navigation lights blinking away in the distance. On a couple of occasions, Collins had had to alter course manually in order to keep their distance from an on-coming vessel before switching back to autopilot. He clearly knew what he was doing and Sam, who even at this late stage was still having misgivings about the venture, was mightily relieved to see it.

So far, everything had gone to plan. The drive down from London to St Margaret's Bay had taken nearly three hours and they had arrived just after midnight. Pulling up in the deserted car park at the beach front, Collins had flashed a torch three times in quick succession. Almost immediately, from out at sea, there came an answering three flashes.

'That's Ron,' Collins grunted. Getting out of the car, he opened the boot and pulled out two sets of waterproof overalls and tossed one to Sam. 'Put that on.'

Minutes later as they stood waiting on the beach, a boat suddenly glided out of the darkness and heaved-to about ten metres offshore. From around the side of the small wheelhouse, a man's head appeared, and he yelled, 'Come on.'

'Here we go.' Collins began wading out through the surf to where the boat lay pitching slightly in the swell. Sam followed along behind. He was waist deep by the time he reached the vessel and Collins, who was already aboard, leaned over and helped him up over the side.

As Sam shrugged out of the waterproofs, he heard Ron

saying. 'When you get back, flash the light and I'll come out and take the boat back to Folkestone. We'll meet up later to sort out the cash.' Swinging his legs over the side, he lowered himself into the water and waded ashore.

Wasting no time, Collins had the boat underway and headed out to sea before his brother had reached the beach. That had been three quarters of an hour ago and now that they were halfway across without encountering any problems, Sam was feeling considerably more relaxed.

It was about thirty minutes later when Collins suddenly tapped Sam's arm and pointed, 'Look, lights. We'll be there in ten minutes or so.'

Straining his eyes, Sam could just make out a smattering of dim lights low on the horizon ahead of them. 'I thought this beach we're going to is supposed to be deserted,' he asked. 'Where are the lights from?'

'The lights are from Calais. Gironde Beach is over there.' Collins pointed over to the starboard side where nothing was visible.

Minutes later, he muttered. 'The shore should be coming into view any time now. Yes, there it is, can you see?'

About two hundred metres away, Sam saw the outlines of the shore with the breaking waves leaving a faint white line. He nodded.

'Right, remember what I told you. The sea is particularly shallow around here so we can't go closer than a hundred metres or so. We'll drop anchor and then I'll take the dinghy ashore, do the business and then start ferrying the cargo out. All you have to do is sit tight until we start getting them aboard.'

'OK.'

'Let's see where our friends are.' Flicking a switch on the console in front of them, he flashed the boat's light. For a moment there was nothing, and then over to their left came an answering flash.

Collins grinned. 'It's all coming together Sammy my boy.' He steered the boat in a bit further before suddenly pulling back on the throttle, bringing it to a stop.

'Hold it like this.'

Waiting until Sam had taken the throttle, he scrambled to the front of the boat and released the anchor. Looking back at Sam, he shouted, 'You can switch switch the engine off now.' Making his way aft, he got hold of the rope holding the dinghy and began hauling it in. When it was alongside, he clambered in, fired up the engine and took off towards the beach.

With nothing to do but wait, Sam sat down, lit a cigarette and stared shoreward trying to make out what was happening. He was uncomfortably aware that they were rapidly approaching the point of no-return. At the moment, all they were guilty of was an unauthorised excursion into another country's territorial waters. But once the first immigrant was onboard it would be a whole different ball game. From that point on they would be illegal people traffickers and facing a long stretch in prison if caught at it.

It took Dave Collins just a couple of minutes to reach the shore. Throttling back as he approached, he let the dinghy beach itself with a slight bump. Jumping out, he hauled it a few metres up the beach and then stood look-ing around for signs of life.

For a few moments, there was nothing. Then he heard the sound of footsteps crunching in the coarse sand and a tall figure suddenly loomed into view. Coming to a stop in front of Collins, the man stared at him before saying, 'I am Michel.' He glanced at his watch and nodded ap-provingly. 'You are exactly on time. Come.' Turning, he started up the beach.

As they neared the top, it gave way to a rocky area that had been worn flat by the elements over the centuries. On it, stood a large lorry around which a crowd of men were standing.

Reaching the lorry, Michel gestured at the men. 'Your cargo.'

Moving over to the immigrants, Collins counted them. There were twenty-five as agreed. Turning to the French-man, he asked curiously, 'Where are they from?'

'These are Iranian. We get them from all over the Mid-dle East but most of them are from Iran.' He sounded totally indifferent. Going over to the lorry's cab, he opened the door and pulled out a large holdall. Walking back, he dropped it at Collins feet. 'Your money.'

Going down on one knee, Collins opened the bag and shone his torch inside. It was crammed with bundles of £50 notes. Picking one up, he riffled through it. 'How much in each bundle?' he asked.

'£5000.'

Tipping the money onto the beach, he counted the contents of one bundle and then the number of bundles

– there were forty-eight of them. Satisfied, he stuffed them back in the bag and then got to his feet. Holding his hand out, he said, 'Good doing business with you.'

'And you.'

Collin's attention switched to the crowd of immigrants who were shuffling around nervously. 'Will you help me to get them onboard the boat?' he asked.

The Frenchman's reply was brusque. 'No. The deal was for me to deliver them to this beach. This I have done. What happens from now is nothing to do with me.' Getting into the lorry, he drove off without further ado.

'Fuck you too,' Collins muttered under his breath. He was alone on the beach with twentyfive extremely uneasy men all staring expectantly at him.

'Do any of you speak English?' he called out.

A figure stepped forward. 'Yes, I do.'

'Good. Would you explain to your friends that I will take them out to the boat, five at a time, on the dinghy. It will take about thirty minutes to transfer you all and then it's across to England. The crossing will take about ninety minutes. Understood?'

The man nodded. Turning to his companions he spoke briefly and then turned back to Collins. 'I have told them.'

'Let's go then.' Waving the men forward, Collins started down the beach.

The transfer took longer than he had expected as quite a few of the immigrants needed chivvying along. Even so, it was no more than forty-five minutes before the last five had been loaded into the dinghy.

Before getting aboard himself, Collins turned and faced the shore. Keying 'one hour' into his phone, he hit the Send key.

Back on the boat, Sam had been getting the immigrants settled. It wasn't really big enough to hold twentyfive men comfortably so he'd had to squeeze them in wherever he could. Already they were beginning to grumble and, given they were each paying £10,000, he couldn't blame them. As he watched the dinghy approach with the last five Iranians, he was wondering where the hell he was going to put them. In the end, three had to sit on the floor between outstretched legs, with the other two sitting at the bow of the boat, their legs dangling over the front.

When they were all aboard, he made his way to the wheelhouse where Collins was getting ready for the return trip. 'I take it you got the money?' he asked.

Collins pointed at the holdall. 'Is the Pope Catholic? I'll show you in a minute. First though, we need to get on our way.'

Minutes later, they were heading out to sea. Turning, Sam looked back at the immigrants. They were a pathetic sight all huddled together, almost ghostly in the faint moonlight peeking through a gap in the clouds.

'You have to feel sorry for these poor sods. What prospects do they have when they get to the UK? No home, no job, nothing.'

'That's their problem.' Collins was unmoved. 'Here, take the wheel a minute.' Picking up the holdall, he opened it and held it out so Sam could see inside. 'There's more money in there than either of us have ever seen. This could be just the start as well.'

Reaching across, Sam pulled out a couple of bundles. 'Fucking hell,' he breathed disbelievingly. Then he dropped the money back in the bag. 'All we have to do now is get back safely.'

Collins laughed. 'Relax. We're nearly home and dry.'

Little did Sam know that while Dave Collins was indeed nearly home and dry, he himself most definitely was not. His fortunes were about to take a very grim turn indeed!

It was the early hours of Sunday morning when something woke Polly Santana from a deep sleep. The passionate lovemaking of the previous evening came back to her and an involuntary shiver ran through her at the memory. Hayes had been a fantastic lover – one of the best she'd ever had.

With the window open for some reason, it was chilly in the room and she reached out for him. Only he wasn't there. According to the bedside clock it was 2.15. Getting up, she grabbed a dressing gown and went in search of him.

Seeing a light shining under the kitchen door to her right, Polly opened it and went in. Sitting at the breakfast bar facing her, Jack Hayes was busy doing something on a laptop.

'What on earth are you up to at this of night?' she asked sleepily.

Looking up in surprise, he smiled ruefully. 'I'm working believe it or not.' Seeing the slightly doubtful look that crossed her face, he explained. 'I'm waiting for someone to contact me with regard to a crime that's due to happen

tonight. I'm going through some case files while I wait –
it'll save having to do it tomorrow.'

'Seriously?'

Hayes nodded. 'It's not unusual. Go back to bed, I
shouldn't be much longer.'

'Well don't be. It's cold in the bedroom and I need
warming up.'

'Is that a fact?' There was a glint in his eyes as he said
it.

'Assuming you're up to it that is! You can't have much
energy left after last night, surely?'

Hayes grinned. 'You reckon? I'm not known as the stud
of Hampstead Heath for nothing you know.'

Polly rolled her eyes. 'Oh please! You're much nicer
when you're modest.' Going back into the bedroom, she
closed the window before getting in bed. Lying on her
back, she thought about the man. Her initial intention
had been to simply fuck him and then move on to the
next one who took her eye. But she was now thinking she
would quite like to see more of him. Polly had never been
one for long-term relationships but the idea of one with
Hayes was beginning to grow on her. With that thought
in her mind, she went back to sleep.

Over in the kitchen, Hayes was becoming increasingly
impatient. The contact was overdue now and he was getting too tired to concentrate on the files. He was checking
his watch for the umpteenth time when his phone suddenly beeped. In the quiet of the early hours, it gave him
a start.

'About fucking time,' he muttered, snatching it up. The

message was brief. 'One hour.'

'Understood,' Hayes texted back. He then called his contact in the UK Border Force. 'It's Jack Hayes. The target will be in position in one hour.' He rang off. It was up to the Border Patrol now.

At long last it was time for some much-needed sleep. If the lady was expecting any more tonight, he thought as he switched off the kitchen light, she was going to be disappointed – he was too knackered.

Three-quarters of an hour into the return journey, Sam was beginning to think they might actually get away with it. The conditions were even better now, the wind having dropped completely leaving a flat calm sea, and the immigrants were all sitting quietly and causing no trouble. He didn't really know what he had been expecting but it definitely wasn't something as straightforward and easy as this.

Just as on the outbound journey, the night was alive with the navigation lights of other vessels and periodically Collins would override the automatic navigation system to avoid getting too close to one. He was in the process of just such a manoeuvre at that very moment and Sam watched as he nudged the wheel to starboard and the lights of the encroaching vessel quickly faded away to their port side.

The danger past, Collins turned his head to Sam. 'Take a look outside will you and check everything is okay.'

Waiting until Sam had left, he flicked a switch on the boat's control console. A grim smile spread across his face; things were about to get interesting. Lighting a cigarette, he leant casually against the side of the wheelhouse and waited for the fun to begin.

Having completed his check, Sam re-joined Collins in the wheelhouse. 'Everything's fine.'

'Good.'

Fifteen minutes later it began. Knowing what to expect, Collins had been keeping a close eye on the radar screen, and so immediately picked up the blip that indicated a vessel moving towards them from the Northeast. Switching his gaze from the screen to the horizon, it wasn't long before he visually identified the vessel from its lights as they grew steadily larger and brighter. It was a couple of miles away and, glancing across at Sam, Collins could see he was unaware of its impending approach. The time had come to make his move.

Turning around to face aft, Collins made a show of checking out the rear of the boat. Suddenly, he muttered worriedly, 'That doesn't look right.'

'What doesn't?' Half expecting something to go wrong at any moment, Sam picked up on it immediately.

'The dinghy. It doesn't seem to be riding as well as it should be.'

Sam followed Collin's gaze to where the little craft was bobbing up and down in their wake. 'It looks all right to me.'

Collins shook his head. 'No there's definitely something not right. It could be that it's deflating – it's a common problem with these inflatables. That fucking brother of mine! I told him to check it out. I'd better take a look. Now listen, this is important. Whatever you do, don't take your eye off the plotter. You must make sure our course doesn't deviate from 187 degrees. If it does, switch over to manual like I showed you and correct it. I'll be as quick as I can.'

Clapping Sam on the shoulder encouragingly, he hurried aft. Following his instructions, Sam kept his attention firmly fixed on the GPS plotter.

Moments later, Collins reached the rear of the boat and began hauling in the dinghy. When he had it alongside, he secured it in place and then, swinging his legs over the side of the boat, lowered himself into it. Heavily laden, the fishing boat was low in the water and so he didn't have far to drop.

Up in the wheelhouse, with his attention split between the plotter and the horizon, Sam was too busy to worry about what his companion was up to. It was only a matter of minutes before he noticed a vessel closing on them rapidly. He could only see its lights but they were getting steadily brighter.

'Fuck, I don't like the look of this,' he muttered. He was just about to call out to Collins when he heard an engine roar to life. Craning his head to see what was going on, Sam was gobsmacked when the dinghy, with Collins sitting at the back, pulled out from the side of the boat. He gaped in astonishment as the little craft raced off in the opposite direction to the vessel that was bearing down on them. Swallowed up by the darkness, it was out of sight in moments.

Looking down at where the holdall of cash had been,

he saw it was gone. Sam was so stunned that he simply couldn't register what was happening. It was only when a powerful searchlight suddenly bathed the boat in bright light that he snapped out of it. With horror, he realised he was on his own and in sole charge of the fishing boat and its illegal cargo.

Shielding his eyes, he could just make out the shape of a large vessel a few hundred metres away on the starboard side.

'This is the commander of Her Majesties cutter Vigilant. Switch your engine off. I intend to board,' an amplified voice boomed out of the darkness.

Dumbstruck, Sam wracked his mind frantically trying to think of something sensible to respond with. He couldn't. Behind him, excited chatter broke out among the immigrants who had hitherto been sitting quietly.

The voice called out again. 'I repeat. Bring your vessel to a halt.'

With no options available to him, Sam swore loudly and bitterly before pulling the throttle lever back. The fishing boat came to a stop and sat there wallowing in the swell.

In a daze now, he watched helplessly as a small boat was launched from the rear of the cutter and sped across the water towards them. Moments later, it was alongside. Two men climbed aboard – one a uniformed officer and the other a crewman. Pushing through the crush of bodies, they made their way to where Sam stood apprehensively in the wheelhouse.

'Are you in charge here?' The officer spoke in a curt,

no-nonsense manner.

Sam nodded resignedly. 'Yeah.'

The man looked around at the mass of immigrants crammed into every available inch of deck space. 'Who are these people and where are you taking them?' The expression on his face told Sam he already had a good idea.

'They're Iranians. We picked them up in France and are taking them to the UK.'

'You're people-trafficking in other words.' The officer stared at Sam coldly. 'Who was in the dinghy? We saw it on the radar.'

Sam swallowed uncomfortably. Knowing he would sound a complete idiot, he was about to explain how he had been abandoned by his partner when the man spoke again. 'Don't bother, I can guess. You've been dropped in the shit, haven't you?' He shook his head contemptuously.

Turning to the crewman, he said, 'Cooper, see if these people are okay.' He watched as the man went round and checked the immigrants.

Sam was having trouble keeping up with events – it was happening so fast. Within little more than half an hour, they had gone from being almost home and dry to being in custody for a serious crime. Except it wasn't "they" but rather "he".

'How did you find us?' he asked, genuinely mystified. 'We kept away from the usual trafficking routes and our GPS signal is switched off.'

The officer gave him an almost pitying look. 'Is that so?

Well, for starters, you happen to be smack bang in the middle of the main trafficking route. Not only that, your GPS signal *isn't* switched off – we've been tracking you with it for the last fifteen minutes. Plus, we had advance notice you were coming. You never had a chance actually.'

'The passengers seem to be fine sir.'

'Okay. Go back to the ship and report the situation here. I'll bring this in.'

Minutes later, they were underway again. This time with the Border Force officer at the wheel. Standing beside him, Sam was trying to make sense of it all. Initially, he'd assumed that Collins's abrupt departure had been because he'd suddenly realised the game was up. Now, in light of what the Border Force man had just told him, it was clear that there was more to it than that. Collins had assured him they would cross the channel well away from the usual trafficking routes and that it would be impossible for them to be tracked. Both assurances had turned out to be false. It was beginning to look as though Collins had recognised early on that Sam was open to exploitation because of his troubling situation at home. He had taken full advantage by using Sam to help carry out the operation and then leaving him to take the rap.

The whole thing was brilliant really, he admitted to himself with a rueful shake of the head. The UK Border Force had rescued twentyfive immigrants, and also had someone to pin it on. So they would be happy. Dave Collins had escaped with the best part of a quarter of a million pounds in his pocket and would also be happy. He, on the other hand, was looking at a lengthy jail sentence.

Sam's thoughts switched to his family. What on earth would Katie do now? He knew she wouldn't be able to manage on what she earned. Despair overtook him then and, for the first time in years, tears came to his eyes. It lasted but a few moments though. He had been brought up in a tough school where self-pity got you nothing. Anger quickly took over at his stupidity in ever getting involved with Collins and then turned to cold rage. 'I'll get you for this you bastard,' he whispered.

Polly Santana woke early. Beside her, Jack Hayes was in a deep sleep. The upper half of his body was uncovered and, once again, she couldn't help but admire his physique. He had it just about right she thought. Lean and muscular without being muscle-bound – something she always found unattractive.

Hayes was out for the count, which was hardly surprising having been up half the night, so she didn't wake him. Picking her clothes up off the floor, she made for the kitchen after a detour to the bathroom. Hungry, she opened the fridge, located bacon and eggs and proceeded to prepare herself some breakfast.

As the bacon and eggs sizzled in the pan, she wondered how the day was going to play out. She herself had nothing planned and she was hoping that Hayes didn't either. The recent spell of fine weather looked set to continue and the thought of going out somewhere for the day appealed to her. It would give her a chance to get to know him better – something, she realised, she really wanted.

She was about to dish up her breakfast when she heard

Hayes lumping about in the bedroom. Smiling, she put more eggs and bacon in the frying pan. She'd yet to meet the man who didn't appreciate having his breakfast cooked for him.

Having had just four hours of sleep, Jack Hayes was tired and irritable. Indeed, he was so tired he had for the moment forgotten all about Polly Santana. So, when he got to the kitchen door a few minutes later and saw her standing there at the cooker, he stopped dead, blinking in surprise. Then the events of the previous evening came back to him.

'I thought you'd be gone by now,' he muttered by way of greeting. Moving over to the fridge, he poured himself a glass of juice and stood there awkwardly.

Assuming he was just out of sorts from the late night, Polly laughed. 'Don't look so grumpy. I'm cooking you a nice breakfast. I don't do that for many men, I can tell you.'

When it was ready, she put the two plates of food on the table, sat down and started eating. After a moment, Hayes sat down opposite and picked up his knife and fork reluctantly. From the way he proceeded to push the food around the plate, it was clear he didn't really want it.

'Aren't you hungry?' Polly asked. 'You should be after last night!'

'No, not really.' He ignored the teasing note in her voice. He wouldn't have done the previous evening, she knew.

Things weren't going the way Polly had hoped. She

tried again. 'I was thinking we could perhaps have a day out and get to know each other better. Maybe a park – it's going to be sunny all day. And after that, well who knows!'

Hayes shook his head. 'Can't do it. I'm going to be really busy today.'

'Not on a Sunday, surely,' she protested.

He shrugged. 'I'm a policeman. Sundays are the same as any other day. Sorry.' He didn't sound as though he were sorry.

At a loss what to say now, and discomforted at his obvious lack of interest, she concentrated on her breakfast. There was an uncomfortable silence while they ate. When he'd finished, Hayes pushed his chair back. 'Thanks for that. Now I'm going to have to ask you to leave.'

Hiding her disappointment, Polly said brightly, 'Never mind, we'll do it another day then.'

'Well …' There was a shifty air about him and suddenly she realised.

'Is that it then?' she demanded. 'You've fucked me and now you want out. Just like that.'

Avoiding her furious glare, he shrugged as if to say, 'You know how it is.'

Polly shook her head disbelievingly. Men just didn't treat her in such a dismissive way

'You fucking bastard. I hope you get the pox and die.' Stalking furiously from the room, she collected her things and stormed out of the flat slamming the door behind her as she went.

Jack Hayes had just made a serious enemy. Polly Santana would come back to haunt him.

Seated on a stool behind the bar, Stan Cooper was reading a newspaper. The saloon in front of him was deserted apart from a couple sitting over by the window, so there was little else for him to do.

Situated close to the clifftop, three miles west of the fishing port of Dymchurch, the Ship Inn was in an idyllic setting and, at this time of the year, was usually packed with ramblers and holidaymakers. The wet weather had put paid to that for the day though.

Glancing out the window, he shook his head at the depressing sight of rain teeming down. It had started early that morning and hadn't stopped since. Stan had been twelve when his family came over to England from Jamaica, and he had never forgotten the constant warmth and sunshine there. Even after forty-five years in the UK, twenty-seven of them running the Ship Inn, he had yet to get used to the unpredictable English weather. He doubted he ever would.

He gave the couple by the window a baleful look. They'd been sitting there for over an hour now and all they'd bought was a drink apiece and a bag of crisps. Increasingly annoyed, he was seriously considering telling them to either buy another drink or fuck off out of it when the front door swung open and in came two men. It had been a long time but Stan recognized them immediately.

'Well I'll be damned,' he exclaimed as they came up to the bar. 'If it isn't Ron and Dave Collins. Where the hell have you two been hiding? It must be six or seven years since I last saw either of you.'

Seating themselves on the other side of the bar, the two men grinned broadly at him.

'Nice to see you again, Stan. Still peddling watered-down beer and dodgy meat pies?' Dave Collins chuckled good humouredly.

'Ever the comedian, I see Dave.' Stan shook his head in mock hurt. 'I heard you'd moved up to London. Back for good now?'

'Nah, just visiting. Me and Ron had business to sort out.'

Stan looked from one to the other. 'You both look dead chuffed so it must have gone very well.' The two men did indeed seem inordinately pleased with themselves.

'What can I get you then?'

'Beer for me.' Dave was studying the menu he had picked up from the bar. 'And I'll have a rump steak with a double helping of chips,' he added.

'I'll have the same,' said Ron. 'And give us the biggest

steaks you've got; we haven't eaten since yesterday evening.'

Stan called the order through to the kitchen. For the
next few minutes they gossiped as the two men waited
for their food to arrive. When Stan's wife and chief cook,
Julie, brought it through, they went over to a table in the
far corner of the room.

Watching them, Stan noticed the furtive way Dave Collins glanced around as if to make sure they couldn't be
overheard.

'I told you, I fucking told you.' He banged the table
gleefully with his fist. 'It won't work you said, far too
risky you said, but it has hasn't it? Over two hundred
grand for one nights work.' His grin stretched from ear
to ear.

Ron inclined his head in acknowledgement. 'I can still
hardly believe you got away with it though. There were
so many things that could have gone wrong.'

His brother laughed. 'Rubbish. The whole thing was
extremely well planned and executed. It went sweet as a
nut.'

The two men had rendezvoused at St Margaret's Bay in
the early hours of that morning. Ron had been waiting
with his pickup and they had quickly stowed the dinghy
in the back. The first glimmer of dawn had been breaking
when they drove away, making for Ron's cottage some
ten miles away. He lived alone there with his dog Barney;
his wife Sue having cleared off years previously due to his
drinking.

Exhausted after the night's endeavours, they had

turned in immediately on arrival, not waking until mid-
day. Ron had offered to rustle up something to eat but
Dave, being well acquainted with his brother's culinary
skills, had suggested they eat at the nearby Ship Inn. Plus,
of course, there was the little matter of a drink or two to
celebrate a very successful venture.

'It certainly went well for us. Not so good for that poor
bastard you left on the boat though.' Ron was serious for
a moment. 'I still don't see why it was necessary to abandon him like that; you could have taken him with you on
the dinghy. The Border Force people would have rescued
the immigrants leaving the two of you to get away. That
would have been that. You'd have got your money, the
immigrants would have made it to the UK and everyone
would be happy.'

'You're forgetting two very important things. Firstly, by
leaving him, I've got his share of the money which dou-
bles my pay-out. Secondly, he takes all the heat leaving
me home and dry.'

'The guy's not going to keep quiet about you though,
is he? What makes you so sure the police won't come
after you?'

'Because they've already got him to pin it on. Anyway,
he was a complete dickhead. He just went along with everything I said without checking for himself. What did he
expect?' Dave shook his head. 'No, someone as dumb as
that deserves everything that's coming to him.' There was
no remorse whatever in his voice.

Ron shrugged. 'Yeah, you're probably right. By the
way, how did you know the Border Force people would

find you?'

Dave grinned. 'That was easy. Just before we left the beach in France, I contacted a policeman I know in London telling him when we would be back in UK waters. He passed that on to the Border Force people. I also kept the boat in the main smuggling route between Calais and Dover where they couldn't miss us anyway. And, just to make absolutely sure, I switched the boat's GPS tracking signal back on when our dumb friend wasn't looking. The Border Force knew we were coming, when we were coming and where we would be. Plus, they could track us by GPS. They couldn't fail to find us.' He tapped his head. 'I told you, I had it planned to the last detail.'

Ron nodded. 'I have to hand it to you. So, what do you intend to do now? Go back to London?'

'Yep. But only for as long as it takes me to find another dickhead. I know I said this was going to be a one-off but there's so much easy money to be made, I'd be an idiot to stop now. I reckon another four trips and I'll be at least a million to the good. Then I'll pack it in and go straight.'

He gave his brother a questioning look. 'What about you? Are you in? All you have to do is arrange the boat and meet me at the beach. For that I'll give you £50,000 in hard cash. That's a cool quarter of a million over five runs. You'll never have to go near a stinking fishing boat ever again.'

Ron chewed thoughtfully on a piece of steak. There wasn't that much to think about really. Steal a suitable boat, hand it over to his brother and then meet him on the way back. There was very little risk to himself, it was Dave who was far more likely to be apprehended. It was a no-brainer.

'I'm in.'

'Great. Let's drink to it.' The two brothers clinked their glasses.

20 Years Later

'Gentlemen.' Gavin Osbourne looked around at the twenty-two men and women sitting around the table in the Cabinet room. The Prime Minister wore a grave expression on his lugubrious face. 'Our situation is not good to say the least. The pilots are on strike, these damned eco-warriors have brought half of London to a standstill with their ludicrous protests, and the economy has just officially gone into recession. As if all that isn't bad enough, an opinion poll published today by the Telegraph has us on twenty-two points; three behind the Labour party. There's a general election in nine months' time and the way things are going, we don't have a chance of winning it.'

'That damned fool Williams hasn't helped matters,' a red-faced man seated on the other side of the table growled angrily. He was referring to Oliver Williams, the Trade Secretary, who had just been exposed for fiddling his expenses in a newspaper sting. The media was having a field day with the story.

'He hasn't,' Osbourne agreed. 'However, it'll blow over

soon enough; that sort of thing always does. I'm more concerned with getting these blasted protestors off the streets. Our seeming inability to deal with this is making us look irresolute.' He fixed the Home Secretary, whose remit it was, with a hard stare. 'Time to dust off the water cannon perhaps?'

His attention switched to Phillip Daniels, the Transport Secretary. 'And with regard to the strikes, I suggest you start banging some heads together if you still want to be in a job come Christmas.' His tone was uncompromising, the threat unmistakable.

Not waiting for a response, he continued, 'Now then, I've heard a report that ….,'

'Excuse me Prime Minister.' Standing in the doorway was a scruffy looking individual dressed in jeans and t-shirt. He couldn't have looked more out of place in those surroundings if he'd tried. 'I need a word with you in private now.' The man's appearance may have been unkempt but his voice was authoritative. If he was at all put out by the almost curt summons, Osbourne didn't show it. Nodding, he got to his feet. Pausing at the door, he turned and surveyed the assembled ministers. 'Please have some answers for me by the time I get back.' From the slight shake of his head as he left the room, he clearly wasn't holding his breath.

'Bloody pipsqueak. Who the hell does he think he is, summoning the Prime Minister of the United Kingdom as though *he* is running the country?' The speaker's voice was angry and resentful.

'Quite so. Whatever's the PM thinking, taking advice

from such an odious little upstart. That's our bloody job. In any case, whatever he's got to say can surely be said in front of us,' Sir Simon Mount, the Foreign Secretary, chipped in. Everything about the man screamed wealth and privilege – the upper-class accent, expensive made-to-measure suit, gold tiepin and confident, relaxed manner. He was far from relaxed today though.

The little tirade was greeted by a chorus of indignation and nods of agreement from around the table. Whoever the scruffy man was, he was clearly extremely unpopular with the ministers.

At that very moment, the man in question was ushering the Prime Minister into his little office just down the hall from the Cabinet room. His name was Dominic Madden and he was the PM's recently appointed Chief of Staff. Although not a ministerial position, it effectively made him the second most powerful man in the country behind the PM.

A political bruiser who took no prisoners, Madden had been brought in by desperate party chiefs in an attempt to arrest the disastrous decline in the Conservative Party's fortunes. In power for nearly fifteen years now, it had become complacent and ineffective thanks to the continuous infighting, incompetence and self-interest that riddled it from top to bottom. It had had been decided that drastic measures were needed in order to restore the party's fortunes and Madden was the man chosen to implement them.

'Well Dominic, what's so important you have to drag me away from a Cabinet meeting?' There was a hint of testiness in the PM's voice. While he accepted the need for Madden's guidance, if it could be called that, he was wary of the man and his methods.

If he noticed, Madden gave no indication. Nor did he apologise – it simply wasn't his way. Instead, he got straight to the point. 'I've just had Sir Richard Curtis, head of MI5, on the line. He informs me that George Davis is in bed with the Chinese.'

'In bed with the Chinese? What on earth are you talking about man?' the PM asked almost fearfully, knowing instinctively he wasn't going to like the answer.

'It seems Davis has been taking payments from Huawei to promote its interests here in the UK. Sir Richard also says it's almost certain that Huawei have approached other people who might be helpful to their cause. I need hardly remind you that if any of this gets out, the press will have a field day and the opposition will be screaming from the rooftops.'

Madden was right as well. The Chinese telecoms company, Huawei, had, for some time, been pushing hard to be the main supplier of equipment for the UK's new 5G network. The government had been considering doing a deal with them but concerns that the Chinese may use the network for espionage and/or sabotage had stopped it finalising anything. A number of other countries had refused to deal with Huawei for the same reasons. It seemed the Chinese were now resorting to underhand methods.

Osbourne shook his head in despair. Prime Minister for just over four years now, he had come into the job with high expectations of being able to arrest the decline in just about every area of public life that had taken place under Conservative administration. To his dismay, things had instead got steadily worse. Hence Dominic Madden being been brought into the power loop. The man cared nothing for convention, he was outspoken and rude, didn't suffer fools, and was brutally direct and to the point. To the chagrin of many, his methods worked.

'Jesus Christ! Davis is in charge of our digital and communications industries.'

Madden nodded. 'Which is why the Chinese have nobbled him.'

'They must have bunged him an absolute fortune to do something so stupid. Surely he knows we'd find out.'

Madden snorted. 'Maybe not so stupid actually. For starters, Sir Richard says it was sheer good fortune that MI5 managed to cotton on to him. Plus, Davis knows perfectly well that should he get found out, given the political situation at the moment, we have no choice but to cover it up. The public can't be allowed to know.' He sighed. 'By rights, the bastard should be put on trial but we're almost certainly going to have to let him get away with it. A deal of some sort whereby he's allowed to skulk off into obscurity to enjoy his ill-gotten gains in return for keeping his trap shut. He's on a winner either way. Makes you sick doesn't it.' His disgust was clear.

'I take it he doesn't know we're on to him yet.'

'No, but he bloody well will do very shortly,' Madden said grimly. For a slightly built man, he could be very menacing when he wanted to be. 'Leave the bastard to me, I'll sort him out. In the meantime, we have to find someone to replace him.'

Osbourne rubbed his eyes wearily. 'Bloody hell. It's just one thing after another isn't it?' Pulling himself together after a moment, he said, 'Well, there's that Huntingdon MP, Sue Martin. I've heard good things of her. Plus, we could do with some more women in the Cabinet for PC purposes.'

Madden rolled his eyes impatiently. 'Fuck political correctness; we simply haven't got time for all that crap now. In any case, I haven't seen or heard anything about the woman that suggests she would be any more effective than the tossers we have in the Cabinet now.'

A genteel man, Osbourne winced at the language. However, he knew he had run out of options. He'd tried his best but it hadn't been good enough. Having agreed to let this coarse man run the show behind the scenes, he had to go along with him now. 'Who do you suggest then?' he replied resignedly.

Madden's response was immediate. 'John Meacher. If you remember, he won the by-election in Ely about four years ago. I've heard such good reports about him that I went up there to see for myself. I have to say I was very impressed with the guy. He's hardworking and gets things done – qualities we could do with a lot more of in there.' He nodded in the direction of the Cabinet room.

Osbourne was incredulous. 'Are you serious? You want to give a man with just four years' experience in a minor constituency a position in the Cabinet? Quite apart from the fact he simply doesn't have enough experience for the job, it would create uproar from those who do. Not to mention from the existing ministers who would take a very dim view.'

'Fuck them. They're useless wankers. If we're to turn this mess around, we're going to have to get rid of most of them to make room for people who know what they're doing. Davis has done us a favour actually; he was going to be one of the first to go.' Madden's response was brutal.

He rolled a cigarette and lit it before continuing. 'Meacher is exactly the type we need. He's tough, takes no crap from anyone, is quite happy to break the rules if necessary, and is extremely popular with his constituents. What impressed me more than anything though, is that his colleagues can't stand him because he shows them up for the idiots they really are.' Madden shot Osbourne a look that managed to convey both amusement and threat. 'Just like me really.'

Osbourne stared down at the man. He was leaning casually back in his chair with both feet up on the desk and wreathed in cigarette smoke. Or was it cigarette smoke? He sniffed suspiciously. Osbourne was no expert in these matters having never smoked or taken an illegal substance in his life, but he had a sudden feeling his Chief of Staff was smoking something stronger than tobacco. Not for the first time, the Prime Minister found himself not knowing quite how to respond to the man. In the end, he muttered a short, 'I'll think about it. Now, I've got to get back to the meeting.' Turning, he left the room.

Expelling a cloud of marijuana smoke, Madden

watched him stride away down the corridor.

'What an idiot,' he muttered contemptuously. 'You don't know it yet pal, but I'm going to get rid of you as well.' Swinging his feet to the floor, he picked up the phone and dialled a number. 'Hi John, it's Dominic. It's time to move. I'm about to drop a bomb on this useless administration and I need you in on the action as discussed. So, listen up; this is what's going to happen …'

'The kitchen sink hasn't been sealed around the edges and leaks, the boiler switches itself on and off, none of the doors fit properly, the front door lock doesn't work, the loft hasn't been insulated, the parquet floor in the hall is already lifting up at the edges, three of the electric sockets don't work, the ceiling in the main bedroom is …'

Seated opposite John Meacher on the other side of his desk, the irate woman was reading from a long list that extended to two pages. She was one of the unfortunate owners of a new house in the notorious Loves Farm Housing Development. Poorly designed and built, literally every one of the houses was plagued with a multitude of faults that ranged from just plain annoying to downright dangerous. In one extreme case, over two hundred faults had been identified. The building firm responsible, Fitsimmon Homes, having taken their money, had quite disgracefully abandoned the owners and were now using every trick in the book to duck responsibility for the deluge of complaints they were receiving.

In desperation, a delegation of the owners had taken

their case to him as the local MP, begging him to do something about it. Most MPs faced with this type of situation would have passed the buck by telling them to contact the warranty provider and, if still no joy, take the builder to court. The buyer would go away, do as their MP suggested and, after a while, realise the futility and expense of taking on a national housebuilding firm. Disillusioned, they would then give up, the housebuilder would make a nice profit, the directors would pocket a fat bonus and the MP would continue doing sweet FA.

John Meacher had a different, more direct, way of doing things. On realising the scale of the problem at Loves Farm, he had immediately initiated an investigation into Fitzsimons's board of directors. He hadn't been at all surprised when it revealed a positive web of corruption – back-handers, gratuitous bonus payments, freebies, etc, etc – all the usual stuff. He had then confronted the firm's managing director and demanded action on behalf of the homeowners. With his own neck on the block and facing an opponent who wasn't as easily intimidated as a cash-strapped and desperate customer, the man had quickly capitulated in return for the incriminating evidence being destroyed. That was fine with Meacher. What the board of directors subsequently got up to was their affair as far as he was concerned. He just wanted justice for the owners. That and the boost to his reputation he would gain as a result –there was a general election looming after all!

Raising his hand, he stopped the woman in full flow. 'Mrs Benson, I am aware of what's been going on at

Loves Farm and the appalling way you have been treated by Fitsimmon. As it happens, I have recently been in contact with the company on the owners behalf and, after a bit of gentle persuasion from me, they have agreed to rectify all the outstanding issues, not just with you but with the entire estate. Work is due to commence next week.'

From the look of surprise on her face, it was clear this was not what Mrs Benson had been expecting. She'd had dealings with officialdom before and it simply didn't work like this. Quick, straightforward resolutions just didn't happen.

'Well, I'll believe it when I see it.' She was clearly unconvinced. 'But if something is actually done, Mr Meacher, you'll have my vote in the election next year. And I say that as a lifelong Labour supporter. There'll be a lot more from Loves Farm as well.' Mrs Benson got to her feet.

Meacher had no sooner ushered her outside when his phone rang. Seeing the name Dominic Madden flash up on the screen, he answered with a touch of trepidation. You never knew what to expect with the man.

'John, I've got good news for you. I've just persuaded the PM to appoint you the new minister for Media and Communications. It's a relatively minor position in itself but the important thing is it gets us another voice in the Cabinet. That'll make six so far. Another six and we'll hold the balance of power. At that point we'll be running the show. Now then ...'

Meacher's mind drifted momentarily. Madden had

promised him a Cabinet posting a while back but he had never thought it would actually happen. Thinking back to where he had been just a few short years ago, he shook his head in wonder at how far he had come. And, he suddenly realised, with the power of a Cabinet minister behind him, he could go a damn sight further. He switched his attention back to Madden just in time to hear him say in that staccato way he had of speaking, 'How soon can you get down here?'

Meacher thought quickly. 'Monday. I'll need a couple of days to tie up some loose ends.'

'Fine. I'll send a car to pick you up first thing Monday morning. In the meantime, I'll arrange an office and somewhere for you to live when you get here. There's plenty of grace & favour apartments for government use; one of those will do for the time being. Oh, by the way,' he added as an afterthought, 'bring that private investigator friend of yours as well. He could be useful.' Madden hung up in his usual abrupt way.

Meacher sat back in his chair still in part shock at what he had just heard. An ambitious man, he had set his sights on getting to the top in politics but to achieve a Cabinet position after just four years as an MP was beyond his wildest dreams. It was almost unprecedented and was proof of the power and influence wielded by Dominic Madden.

He buzzed the intercom on his desk. 'Tom, can you come in?'

Seconds later, the door to his assistant's office opened and a slim young man in his late twenties entered. 'You look like you've just won the lottery,' he said, eyeing the delighted look on his boss's face.

Meacher laughed. 'Not quite that good but it'll do for now. Believe it or not, you're looking at the new Minister for Media and Communications.'

Tom Guppy's eyes widened. 'Really. Fucking hell, you'll be Prime Minister soon at this rate.'

'One step at a time my old son. All things are possible though.' Grinning broadly, Meacher looked like the cat who'd got the cream. He related the conversation he'd just had with Dominic Madden before saying, 'Now listen, I have to be in London on Monday. That leaves me what's left of today and tomorrow to sort things out here. I've got a meeting at Addenbrookes Hospital this afternoon and a constituency meeting tomorrow morning, both of which I can manage. Everything else, I'm afraid, I'm going to have to leave to you.'

Guppy nodded. 'Shouldn't be a problem boss.' He gave Meacher a slightly askance look. 'You're not winding me up, are you?'

Meacher smiled. 'No.'

'You'll be spending most of your time in London now then.'

'Definitely. I'll still be having my surgeries here and be available to deal with any serious issues but otherwise I'll be in London.'

'Media and communications, you say. With my background in IT, I could be useful to you there,' Guppy said thoughtfully. 'I presume you're going to take me with you. You're definitely going to need people you can trust.

Who better than me?'

'I was hoping you'd say that. But I want you to stay here for the time being and get things ship-shape. When I've got the lay-of-the-land down there, I'll send for you.'

'Sounds good boss. I know some brilliant clubs in London from my university days; I'll have to take you round some of them,' Guppy said with a chuckle.

Meacher rolled his eyes. 'Yeah, I can just imagine. Women, booze and illicit substances, and those'll be the decent ones. Just the thing for a Cabinet minister. No, I think I'll probably have to pass on that.'

'You're getting old boss.'

Meacher was about to fire off a sharp retort when he noticed the time. 'Christ, I'm supposed to be at Addenbrookes in half an hour.' Shrugging into his jacket, he grabbed his briefcase and hurriedly made for the door. 'See you later.'

There was a glint in Tom Guppy's eyes as he watched Meacher go. Re-entering his own office, he sat down at his desk and began preparing a list of things that had to be done before the move to London. Office administration was not one of Meacher's strong points, and the efficiency with which he ran his constituency office was largely down to Guppy's organisational skills. The sooner he followed his boss to London the better – Meacher would never manage without him.

Tom Guppy had another agenda, which also required him to be in London. This was something John Meacher knew nothing about – yet!

List completed, he lit a cigarette and leaned back in his

chair. There was a hard expression on his face as he murmured, 'It's all coming together.'

Seated at the kitchen island, Jack Hayes was eating his lunch. Comprising two hard-boiled eggs, a tuna & lettuce sandwich, a handful of mixed nuts and a glass of freshly squeezed lemon juice, it provided everything his body needed in the way of nutrients and none of the things it didn't. Open in front of him as he ate was a copy of the Guardian – newspaper of choice for wet-behind-the-ears liberals, socialists and other assorted headcases. Full of left-wing and politically correct claptrap, much of it was so preposterous he actually found it quite an entertaining read.

Hayes had done well for himself since leaving the police force. He hadn't had much choice in the matter as it turned out, his superiors having finally had enough of his extracurricular dealings with the criminal fraternity. Luckily for him, the force was by that time being run by people for whom image was all – concepts such as duty and integrity were way down the list. So instead of ending up in jail as he should have done, he was instead allowed to leave quietly on grounds of "health". He was even given a nice payoff. Nor was he sorry to go. Things had changed a lot from when he'd first joined. In those days, catching criminals and protecting the public was the priority. Then the PC brigade began to take over and it wasn't long before issues such as race, gender, beliefs, religion and sexual orientation were being given equal importance.

Hayes took with him with a wealth of experience and some extremely useful contacts, both inside and outside the force. In the four years since leaving, he had established himself as a very successful and sought-after private investigator.

Lunch finished, he was stuffing the newspaper in the rubbish bin where it belonged when his phone rang. 'Hi Jack. John Meacher here.'

'Hello John,' he said in surprise. It had been a while since he'd last heard from the man.

'Listen Jack, I need to see you - today if possible.' As always, Meacher got straight to it.

'Why, what's up?' Hayes asked curiously.

'I'd rather tell you face-to-face.'

'Where are you - Ely?'

'No, no, I'm here in London. Not far from you actually.'

'Well, as it happens, I'm not doing anything at the moment that can't wait. Why don't you come round now?'

'Brilliant; I always could rely on you Jack. I'll be right over.' With that, he hung up.

Hayes stared at his phone quizzically for a moment before putting it down. He hadn't missed the note of anticipation in Meacher's voice. There was something was afoot!

Fifteen minutes later, he answered the door to see Meacher standing on the doorstep with a big grin on his face.

'John, nice to see you again. Come in.' Hayes put on his best smile. The man was one of his most valued customers. Leading the way through to the kitchen, he waved Meacher to a chair. 'Can I get you a drink?'

'A cold beer would go down well.'

Going over to the fridge, Hayes got two beers out. Opening them, he handed one to his guest. 'Well, John. You look very pleased with yourself, I must say.'

About to put the bottle to his lips, Meacher suddenly set it down again. He was in a state of high excitement and clearly couldn't wait to get his news out. 'You'll never believe this Jack, I can still hardly believe it myself,' he said wonderingly.

'Believe what?'

'You're looking at a member of the Cabinet.'

Hayes's jaw dropped in astonishment. 'Seriously? Since when?'

'Since Friday. Dominic Madden's persuaded, or perhaps I should say told, the PM to make me minister for Media and Communications.'

'Have they gone off their heads?' What do you know about any of that?'

Meacher laughed. 'Fuck all but then what do any of them know. That's why Cabinet ministers have legions of advisors to tell them what to say and do.'

'I'll be damned.' Hayes shook his head. 'When do you start?'

'Already have. I came down from Ely yesterday. Madden's fixed me up with somewhere to stay and I've been getting myself organized. I'm going over to see him at No 10 when I leave here.'

'Well, I suppose congratulations are in order. I just hope you know what you're getting yourself into though. That place is the proverbial nest of vipers.'

Meacher snorted scornfully. 'You know me Jack. I'm as big a viper as any of them.' He picked up the beer bottle and emptied it in one long draught. 'Right, it's time we went.'

'We?'

'Yes, Madden wants to see you as well. Seems he has something in mind for you. He knows how useful you've been to me.'

'You don't say!' Despite instinctive misgivings, Hayes was interested. While involvement with sharp operators like Madden invariably presented risks, it could also present opportunities. He had nothing to lose by seeing what was on offer.

'Let's not keep him waiting then.'

The little park was in a lovely setting. Bounded by woods on either side, it faced a steep cliff that looked out over the sea. Seagulls soared in the clear blue sky and cows grazed peacefully in the field behind.

Surrounded by all that natural beauty, the man had eyes for one thing only though – the youngsters in the playground over to his left.

Seated on a wooden bench no more than fifty metres away, he gave every impression of someone just out to enjoy the scenery. The baseball cap pulled low over his eyes hid his real purpose – ogling the little children. Usually, the mothers spent most of the time glued to their phones, which made it a lot easier for him to eyeball those lithe little bodies unnoticed. Today, though, they were discussing something between themselves and it wasn't long before one of them glanced over in his direction and then muttered something to the others. As one, they turned and stared at him.

It was time to go. Sighing with disappointment, the man got to his feet and slowly shuffled away. His leg was particularly painful today and he grimaced as he stumbled along the uneven path that led to the woods. The route was popular with dogwalkers and ramblers but few of them ever acknowledged him as they passed. There was an undefinable something about him that made people avert their gaze and hurry on.

Entering the woods, he relaxed a bit. Away from prying and suspicious eyes now, he felt safer, more secure, in the relative darkness. Of course, there was nothing for *him* to see and he shook his head at the unfairness of it. Reaching the fallen oak tree in the middle of the wood, he sat down in the seat someone had carved out with a chainsaw. He usually had to stop here to ease the pain in his leg. He wasn't supposed to be on it at all but the playground drew him like a magnet. It was an urge beyond his control.

Getting back on his feet after a few minutes rest, he continued through the wood and came out on the edge of a field in which shoots of barley were just beginning to emerge. The path continued round the field, through another little wood before eventually opening into a narrow lane. At the top of the lane was the main street that ran through the little coastal town of Mundesley. The first bungalow on the left, set back from the neighbouring houses, was where he lived alone with his thoughts.

Entering the house, he went into the kitchen at the rear. Putting the kettle on, he looked out over the back garden while he waited for it to boil. Bounded by a picket fence, it was small but beautifully tendered with well stocked flowerbeds, a neatly trimmed lawn and a small pond in one corner. The birds loved it and so did he, particularly in the summer months when he could sit out there with his laptop and look at his pictures and videos.

Carrying his mug of tea, the man went over to the table at the far end of the room. Sitting down, he picked up a newspaper and flicked through it idly while sipping the brew. After a while, the old familiar urge crept up on him and he reached out for the laptop. Only it wasn't there! Strange! He would have sworn he'd left it on the table before going out. His memory must be playing tricks on him again. Maybe he'd put it in the drawer under the table? He was just opening it when he heard a voice behind him.

'This what you're looking for?'

Standing in the kitchen doorway was a tall figure clad entirely in black – the balaclava that concealed his face was black as well.

The man nearly fell off his chair as he jerked round in shock. Apprehension came into his eyes as he saw the masked man was holding his laptop.

'Who are you?'

The stranger ignored him. Tossing the laptop aside, he moved forward. There was something menacing in his slow, deliberate steps.

Scrabbling to his feet, the man edged backwards in alarm until he was brought up short by the wall.

Coming to a stop a few feet from him, the masked man produced a photograph and held it out. Of poor quality, it showed a young boy who could have been aged anything between eight and twelve. He had a surly, defiant expression on his face.

'Do you remember him?' he demanded.

The pervert stared at the image helplessly. How could he remember? There had been so many over the years.

'No, of course you don't.' The man's voice was thick with disgust. 'Well, let me refresh your memory. His name was Sam Clark. A frightened ten year-old boy who was in your care. You sexually abused him, you wicked bastard. And many others as well.'

'W-w-what are you going to do?' Even as he stammered the words, the man knew what was about to happen. His bulging eyes saw the bone handled knife in the stranger's right hand and, losing control, he wet himself in his terror. Falling to his knees, he begged, 'Please don't. I couldn't help it, you see. It was the boys' fault, they always …'

'Rot in hell, you foul creature. This is for Sam Clark.' The man's eyes were cold and pitiless as he raised the knife and stepped forward.

The story broke the following week, making the front pages in the local Norfolk papers and several of the nationals. The police report had merely said the man had been stabbed to death. In reality, the manner of his killing had been considered too horrific to publicise.

According to the story, the man's name was Thomas Lloyd. He had, for many years, run the Shirley Heights Boys Home in North London. Arrested for repeated abuse of the boys in his care, Lloyd had been sentenced to a term of fifteen years in prison. The judge had described him as a callous and calculating individual who'd shown no remorse for the incalculable hurt and distress he had caused to the innocent youngsters. While in jail, he had been attacked by other inmates on several occasions, one of which had left him with a permanently damaged leg. Lloyd had been released after serving just under half his sentence and given a new identity for his own protection. Police enquiries were ongoing regarding the circumstances of his death.

Local opinion in Mundesley was damning; typical comments being: 'He was a creepy old man with horrible eyes,' 'You could tell there was something wrong there,' 'I would cross the street to avoid him,' 'Even the dog was wary of him,' 'Burn in hell bastard,' and 'Good riddance.'

Located in Parliament Street, just two hundred metres from 10 Downing Street, the Red Lion was a well-known London watering hole. Popular with tourists, journalists and, of course, politicians, the tavern dated back to 1749 and had even been frequented by a young Charles Dickens.

In an alcove, away from eavesdroppers, John Meacher and Jack Hayes waited for Dominic Madden to show up. They had been on the point of leaving Hayes's place for No 10 when Madden had phoned and suggested they meet at the Red Lion instead. Keenly anticipating his first visit to the UK's seat of power as an executive member, Meacher had been a bit put out.

Within minutes of their arrival, Madden came bustling in and stood there for a moment staring round to locate them. He was dressed in his usual jeans and t-shirt and looked more like a tourist – a scruffy one at that – than anything else.

After introducing Madden to Hayes, Meacher immediately asked, 'Why here instead of No 10?' He was still peeved.

Madden shook his head. 'Sorry, I've just found out that my office has been bugged. They've finally realised what I'm up to and are starting the fightback. Not that it'll do them any good.' His voice was contemptuous. 'So, until I've buried the bastards, we'll have to conduct our meetings in places like this.'

Gazing around at the convivial surroundings, Jack Hayes laughed. 'Well, I can think of worse places to meet.' He became more serious. 'You can use that to your advantage, you know. As long as they're unaware that you know you've been bugged, they'll take more or less everything you say in there as gospel. You'll be able to feed them false information and have them believe all sorts of rubbish.'

Madden smiled grimly. 'Your mind works in the same devious way that mine does, I see.' He took a swig of his beer. 'Now then, before I update you on developments John, how much have you told Jack here about our plans?'

'Only that we intend to get rid of the majority of the existing Cabinet members and replace them with people of our choosing – people who are capable of doing the job properly.'

Madden nodded. 'To which I would add by whatever means necessary – the rulebook is out the window.' He looked at Hayes. 'Which is where you come in Jack. A man with your talents and contacts could be very useful to us. Are you interested?'

'That depends on what you want me to do and what I

can expect to get out of it,' Hayes replied noncommittally.

'It's very simple. I need you to dig up dirt on certain individuals that I can use as a means of persuasion.'

'And what's in it for me?'

'Job satisfaction. You'll have the great pleasure of knowing you've played an important part in getting the country back on its feet.' Madden laughed at the pained expression that crossed Hayes's face.

'Okay, okay. My backers are extremely wealthy men and will pay handsomely for information that helps us achieve our objective. We'll go into the details later but, for now, be assured I will make you a very rich man. That sound better?'

'Well, you've stopped talking bollocks at least.' Hayes said dryly. 'Why am I so honoured though? There must be people within the government you can use.'

'Of course there are. But it's precisely because they work for the government that I can't trust them. I need someone who's independent, outside the system. Someone like yourself.'

'I assume you've had me checked out.'

'The report is sitting on my desk right now and very interesting reading it is too.' Madden gave him a hard stare. 'You certainly don't believe in playing by the rules, do you?'

'Rules are for losers. If everyone followed them, so would I. But they don't, do they?' Hayes replied pointedly.

A faint smile crossed Madden's lips. 'Touché. Just so

we're clear – your methods don't concern me as long as you get results. So, can we count on you?'

Seeing no reason to say no at this stage, Hayes nodded, 'Could be interesting.'

'Excellent.' Madden nodded in satisfaction and took another sip of his beer. 'Right, the current situation is this. There are twenty-two ministers in the Cabinet and we need at least twelve of them pulling in our direction. We already have John here and the PM onside, so that leaves ten. There are another four who are sympathetic to our aims and who I consider to be worth their place. So now we're down to six. I've made a list of the remaining ministers and identified the ones I think are least likely to put up a fight. I'll term them the "probables" because they'll be easy to get rid of. The rest are "possibles" who'll be more difficult, so we'll leave them to last.'

He looked at Hayes. 'Now, we're not going to get shot of any of them just by asking nicely. We're going to have to give them a fucking good reason to move their asses. One they can't fight. This is where your "talents" come into play.'

Hayes screwed up his face thoughtfully. 'Well, it's almost certain that at least six out of sixteen politicians, wherever you look, will have something in their past they won't want making public. Will it be enough to make them give up a ministerial position though? The job itself doesn't pay that much but you know as well as I do, it's what it leads to that makes it so valuable. It's a stepping-stone to where the real money is. Highly paid positions in major corporations, the lecture circuit, book deals, the

House of Lords – it's the proverbial licence to print money. They won't give that up without a fight, believe me.'

Meacher spoke up. 'No, of course they won't. We're well aware of that. That's why, should it prove necessary, we'll use the nuclear option. And by that, I mean fitting them up with something that has the potential to destroy them. For example: theft of public funds, taking bribes, sexual shenanigans, etc, etc.'

'Exactly.' Madden slid a sheet of paper across to each of them. 'This is the list of all the Cabinet members and how I see their position. I've highlighted in green the ones already onboard, in pink, the probables, and in red, the possibles.'

Turning to Hayes, he said, 'Start with the names highlighted in pink and see what you can dig up on them; I've no doubt there'll be plenty. Then we can get the ball rolling. Once we've tipped the balance of power our way, it won't take long to get rid of the awkward fuckers.' Madden indicated the names highlighted in red. 'Once we've done that, we can then make a start on winning the public round by introducing the policies they've been crying out for.'

'What do you have in mind then?' Hayes asked curiously. 'Whatever it is, it'll have to be bloody good to get you out of the mess you're in at the moment. To be honest, I don't see how you can.'

'Well, absolutely the first thing is to stop the criminal waste of public funds that has been going on for years. The most obvious example of this is the insane foreign aid budget. Fifteen billion pounds every year doled out to all and sundry around the world while public services here are cut to the bone. That's number one on the list. Number two is the ridiculous salaries paid to public officials – hundreds of thousands a year in many cases. We'll end it by introducing a cap of £100,000. Nobody needs to earn more than that, politicians included. We'll also bring the BBC down to size by doing away with the licence fee. Four billion a year they get and for what? Left-wing bias, repeats, banal game and reality shows, all of which are available on the commercial channels for free. And then there's the fucking royal family – another huge drain on the public …'

'Dominic darling. Fancy finding you in a public house of all places!' In full flow, Madden was interrupted by an extremely attractive woman who had appeared out of nowhere and was standing to the side of Hayes. There was amused sarcasm in her voice.

Glancing up at her, Madden said rather curtly, 'Hello Pol.' He didn't sound particularly pleased at being interrupted.

If she was put out, she didn't show it. Ignoring his companions, she laughed. 'Scheming again? What are you planning on saving us all from this time?'

'Nothing that concerns you my dear. I'm in the middle of a meeting so do me a favour and piss off.'

'Patronising fucker.' Smiling, she leaned down and patted him affectionately on the cheek. 'Where would we all be without you?' Answering her own question, she chuckled, 'Probably in a much safer place. Don't forget our appointment on Saturday is for 7.30. You were late last time. Bye.'

Meacher watched her go wide-eyed. 'Who is *she*? I wouldn't mind an appointment with her myself!'

'She's my fitness trainer, I've been using her for a few months now.' Madden tapped his stomach. 'She's good, I must admit. I've lost over a stone already.' He looked at Meacher's flabby torso critically. 'Wouldn't be a bad idea to get yourself in shape actually.'

Meacher grinned. 'I will if it's with her. Can I have her number?'

Madden shook his head irritably. 'For fuck's sake, can we get on. Now, as I was saying, the policies I've mentioned are just some of many that will enable us to make huge savings. We'll then have money to invest in public services, such as the NHS and the police. Crime in this country is out of control and we'll fix that by increasing police presence on the streets and introducing sentences that will actually deter criminals instead of making them laugh out loud. Reintroducing the death penalty is just one of the ways we'll do that. Other policies will include bringing in strict controls on immigration, beefing up regulation of investment and pension funds, and modernising our antiquated political system so it's fit for purpose.'

He was about to say more when Hayes stopped him by holding up his hands. 'Okay. I'm with you on all of that. If you can get it done, the public will be as well – apart from maybe the royal family. Don't forget, they bring in millions from tourism.'

Madden scoffed. 'Don't make me laugh. Tourists don't come to see the royals; they know bloody well they have more chance of seeing the man on the moon. They come for the history, to see the palaces, the crown jewels, the priceless works of art, the Tower of London. We could get rid of every single member of the royal family, save untold millions, and the tourists would still keep coming, year after year.'

'You may be right but I have my doubts as to whether the public will agree.'

'The royal family is a minor issue,' John Meacher broke in, impatience in his voice. 'The point is, if we can get these policies introduced in time for them to start taking effect before the general election next year, we should be able to turn things around. Everything hinges on that.'

'It all sounds great in theory but don't forget you'll be up against some powerful people,' Hayes said doubtfully.

'And most of them will also have skeletons in the cupboard.' Madden was contemptuous. 'I'm not underestimating them but they can be beaten. And I'm the man to do it.'

Not for the first time, Hayes noticed his habit of saying "I" rather than "we" and couldn't help but wonder if Madden was perhaps on some sort of personal crusade. He really wasn't sure what to make of the man. He was either mad, bad, inspired or a combination of all three.

Madden picked up his glass and emptied it. 'Well, I've got to get back now. When you've finished here John, come over to No 10 and I'll show you round. I know you're itching to see it.' He looked at Hayes. 'There's no point you coming; security wouldn't allow you in. In any case, I don't want anyone there to know we're working together. So, you've got to keep well away from the place.'

Hayes shrugged. 'Suits me.'

'Right, let me know when you've got something.' Getting to his feet, Madden shook hands with both of them and left.

When he had gone, Meacher turned to Hayes. 'Well, what do you think Jack?' His voice was serious.

Hayes stared at down the table for a few moments before answering carefully. 'I don't know what to think to be honest. Okay, the country is stuck with a rotten government that has to go – I get that. And, as things stand, the usual way of doing it, i.e. a general election, isn't going to work because it will put a Marxist rabble in power and thus make things even worse. So, the only way is to change the key figures in the government from within. I get that as well. What I'm not sure about, however, assuming it goes to plan, is the fact we'll end up with a Cabinet full of puppets whose strings are pulled by Dominic Madden. Effectively, he will be running the country. Will he be any better than what we've got now?'

'Well, he couldn't be any worse,' Meacher muttered with feeling.

'And have you thought about what might happen if it all turns to shit? You're playing a dangerous game here John. These people may be useless at running the country but they are far from useless when it comes to looking after their own interests. You surely aren't expecting them to just roll over for you?'

'Listen, Madden is a bit of a loose cannon, I grant you. And yes, he has some strange ideas and yes, he upsets a lot of people. However, I honestly believe that all he wants to do is to clean up politics and get the country back on its feet. I don't think he has a hidden agenda, unlike most of the bastards out there.'

From his tone, it was clear Meacher had no doubts regarding his mentor's integrity.

'And to answer your second question, yes of course I realise it could all go pear-shaped. But it's not as likely as it may seem. You need to know that Madden himself is just a pawn in this game, as are you and I. There are some very powerful people indeed behind him. I'm talking about billionaire bankers and industrialists whose main interest in life is making money. Thanks to the serial incompetence of this government they are, instead, losing it and they're not happy. They've decided things simply cannot go on as they are any longer. Dominic Madden is their chosen weapon of attack and they'll ensure he gets all the support he needs. That makes him a very powerful individual.'

'Do you know who any of these backers are?' Hayes asked curiously.

'No and I don't want to. As you so rightly said, this is a dangerous game and I don't want to be involved any more than necessary.' Meacher leaned across the table and spoke in a low voice. 'Listen Jack. We're two of a kind, you and me. We've both come from nowhere and we can both go a lot further. For me, Madden is the key.

It's only because of him that I am now a Cabinet minister. Without his support, I'd still be scratching my arse in a backwater constituency and likely stay there. He's told me that unless someone better shows up, I'm his favourite to be Prime Minister in time for the general election next year. It may happen, it may not. But I intend to be around just in case it does.' With a shrug, he added. 'Anyway, if it does all turn to shit, I won't have lost anything.'

'Well, I still think you're riding for a fall but I wish you luck.'

On leaving the Red Lion, Polly Santana walked across the road and into a coffee shop directly opposite. Sitting down at a table by the window, she had a good view of the pub. Ordering a coffee she didn't really want, she waited.

She'd been in the pub to meet a client who hadn't shown up. Giving up eventually, she had been on her way out when she'd spotted Dominic Madden at a table with two men. He was a good client who had put a lot of custom her way. More than that though, she liked him. His grumpy, irascible manner and complete lack of social graces made her laugh, and she always looked forward to their weekly workout sessions.

One of the men she'd never seen before but there had been something about the other one, who'd sat with his back to her as she approached, that was vaguely familiar. While talking with Madden, Polly had glanced at him curiously and, with a start, realised who it was. The forehead was lined now, the beard flecked with grey, but it was definitely Jack Hayes; the policeman she had fallen for, and who had used and then rejected her so cruelly, all those years ago.

Hayes had returned her glance but if he remembered her, gave no indication of it. He seemed pre-occupied and had immediately looked away.

Dominic Madden had been a client for over a year now and, as was so often the case with her clients, it hadn't been long before he came to see her as a soulmate – someone impartial he could share his problems with. Their sessions were usually in the early evening and he sometimes came straight from No 10 literally steaming with frustration and anger. The first time, she'd been quite shocked at the language and indiscretions he'd come out with.

Polly had dealt with all kinds of people over the years and there was little she hadn't experienced at one time or another. Sexual advances were not uncommon, and not just from the men! Some people she liked, some she didn't, some she felt sorry for, and some she was attracted to. Madden was different though. He was such a complex and unpredictable character, she really couldn't find a box to put him in. In fact, she doubted such a box even existed!

She had been sitting there for ten minutes or so when she saw the three men leave the pub. They exchanged a few words before Madden and the other man headed off up the street. Polly watched Hayes pull out his phone, make a brief call and then stride away in the opposite direction. She was tempted to follow but didn't want him to spot and maybe recognise her. There was something going on and, with Madden being involved, there was a good possibility it was something significant. Something that might just present her with the chance of getting even with Jack Hayes. But first, she had to discover what they were up to, and the only way she was going to do that was get it from the man himself.

Madden had never mentioned his personal life to her, and Polly had wondered more than once about his sexual inclinations. He had never made a move on her, which was fine as she wasn't in the least bit attracted to him. That was maybe going to change on Saturday evening though. She wanted information and knew a very good way to get it.

Getting to her feet, she said to herself with a chuckle, 'Well, Polly my girl, I think maybe your next session with Mr Madden will be rather different than usual. I hope he's ready for it.'

'Gentlemen, I'm sure you'll join me in welcoming a new member to our team, John Meacher. John is our MP for Ely in Cambridgeshire and will be taking over from George Davis as minister for Media and Communications.'

It was Thursday morning, two days after his meeting with Madden and Hayes, and Meacher was sitting in on his first Cabinet meeting. Madden had warned him not to expect a rapturous reception and so it proved.

The lukewarm round of applause that followed the Prime Minister's introduction indicated clearly enough that many, if not most, of the ministers had reservations, and maybe even suspicions, about him and his sudden and unexpected elevation to the Cabinet.

Meacher couldn't have cared less. Getting to his feet, he looked around the table before saying simply, 'Thank you, Prime Minister.' Then he seated himself again.

'I also would like to welcome you to the Cabinet. A word to the wise, however, old chap. As a new and um… inexperienced MP, I think it would behove you to keep a low profile until you get the hang of the way things are done around here. In the meantime, us old hands will be more than happy to advise you as best we can.' The speaker was Sir Simon Mount, the Foreign Secretary. His plummy upper-class voice was pompous and reeked of condescension.

Meacher fixed the man with a cool stare. 'Thank you. However, I am not here to keep a low profile. I am well aware of the way things "are done around here" as you put it. It's why we're up shit creek without a paddle. It may interest you to know I'm not just some wet-behind-the-ears MP from a backwater constituency. I'm here to introduce some much-needed expertise, not to mention common sense, to this Cabinet.' Pausing, he stared around the table again. There was a warning note in his voice as he continued. 'Things simply cannot carry on as they are. Anyone here who is unable or unwilling to rec-ognise that fact will very soon have to make room for someone who does.' He nearly added, 'And if they won't do it voluntarily, they will have to do it involuntarily,' but thought better of it – he'd said enough already!

There was a stunned silence in the room as the assem-bled ministers digested not just his words, but the meas-ured and provocative way they had been delivered. They were both a statement of intent and a clear threat. Not at all what they had been expecting from a new minister, and a junior one at that, on his first day in the job.

'Oh, I see. You've been an MP for what, four years, and already you think you know better than us. May I remind you that I have been an MP for thirty-three years now, seven of which have been as a Cabinet minister. I've forgotten more than you'll ever know, as do most of the people in this room. How dare you lecture us. You clown.' Mount glared furiously at Meacher.

There was a rumble of agreement from around the table. Meacher shrugged his shoulders and ignored them. His scorn was clear. Which, of course, riled them all the more.

'Gentlemen please, this is no way to carry on.' Osbourne had to raise his voice to make himself heard over the hubbub. As tempers began to cool and the commotion died down, he directed an irritated 'was that really necessary?' look at his new minister.

After that, the Cabinet meeting proceeded much as it usually did. Of the various issues that were discussed, just one was of interest as far as Meacher was concerned. This was the case of a Conservative MP, Keith Jones, who had extended and modernised a second home and then claimed the costs back on his expense account. Needless to say, the discussion revolved around how best to hush it up. As ever, it was their default response. The MP concerned would be censored but keep his job.

Meacher couldn't contain his exasperation. Jumping to his feet, he exclaimed, 'Do you people never learn? It's as likely as not that the press will get hold of this at some point and then we'll have two scandals to face – the original one and the subsequent cover-up. It's what the public have come to expect and is a major reason why they regard us with such contempt.'

'Ah ha, the new boy doesn't agree! Well, what do you

suggest then? Treat us to some of this expertise and common sense we apparently don't have,' Sir Simon Mount drawled patronisingly.

'I think we should just own up to it and sack the man. Not only would that make other MP's think twice, it would go some way to restoring public trust. And that is something we simply have to do to have any chance of the winning the election next year.'

Mount lowered his head to the table and groaned, 'Dear God, I can't believe I'm hearing this.' Looking across at Meacher, he said patiently, as though explaining something to a child. 'Listen, you, me and everyone here in this room represent the Establishment. Out there,' he jabbed a finger at the window, 'is the public. Two separate entities. We make the rules and they follow them – it's as simple as that. Now for it to work, they need to trust us. And if we admit to every little peccadillo, they won't. So now and then, we have to sweep things under the carpet. It's just the way the system works. Perhaps you know a better way! If so, why don't you enlighten us?'

Meacher could see there was no point in arguing with the man. He was an establishment figure through and through, and could clearly see no further than the end of his nose. He would have preferred to ignore Mount completely but he could see the entire table was waiting to hear his response.

'No, no, I wouldn't presume to tell a man of your vast experience how to do things. After all, you've been a member of the Cabinet for seven years and during that time, you've not only been Foreign Secretary but Home Secretary and Defence Secretary as well. Three very important and influential positions. Is it coincidence then I wonder, that these same seven years have seen this government become a byword for corruption, scandal and incompetence on a scale that has rarely, if ever, been witnessed before. The public hold us in utter contempt and the opposition, led by a mad Marxist throwback who even the Russians find amusing, are running rings around us. As things stand, we haven't a chance of winning the general election next year. So, Sir Simon, you carry on as usual. You and your kind are doing an admirable job.' With that, Meacher got to his feet, nodded to Gavin Osbourne and left the room.

Jack Hayes was a resourceful man; it was an essential requirement for a private investigator. His time in the police force had given him access to those resources. While he had always enjoyed the challenges of being a policeman and did the job to the best of his ability, he had always known that one day his "extracurricular' activities" would catch up with him and he would have to leave the force. He had, therefore planned for it. Deciding that when the day eventually came, working as a private investigator would be his best option, he set about building an extensive network of contacts and of people who owed him favours. He did this so successfully that by the time he left the police, he had access to the Police National Computer, British Intelligence Services, the European Police Office (Europol) and the International Criminal Police Organization (Interpol).

So, when he got to work on Dominic Madden's list of "probables" in search of compromising evidence, it didn't take him long to get results. Within a week, he had uncovered evidence that five of them had been involved in dodgy dealings of one kind or another.

One had been caught speeding and got his wife to claim she was the driver thereby avoiding penalty points on his licence that would have seen him banned from driving. Another, Martine Miller the Culture Secretary, had been fiddling her expenses claims. A more serious case involved the Secretary of State for Work and Pensions, John Lowe. He had breached anti-money laundering legislation by failing to declare a fifty percent interest in a property firm. This had enabled him to buy five luxury flats with the help of a bulk discount from the property developer. Then there was Steven Griffiths, the Transport Secretary. Hayes had discovered that the man had sent a series of texts of a sexual nature to a constituent. Lastly, there was Alister Byrne, Scottish Secretary, who had held secret trysts in hotels with Romanian rent boys. As far as Hayes could make out, Byrne's wife had no knowledge of what he had been up to. That was something that could be easily rectified, though. He could find nothing on the others.

Faced with the details being made public and/or prosecution, none of them Hayes knew, would be able to resist the call to stand down. While replacing them with his own men still wouldn't give him the majority he needed, Madden would at least then have a powerful faction within the Cabinet that could not be ignored. In the meantime, Hayes could get to work on the "possibles".

He was holed up in the little office at the rear of his flat. The window looked out over ranks of high-rise buildings and when the weather was dank and overcast, as it was today, it was a depressing sight. The front view wasn't much better. It never failed to amaze him that despite those views and having just two bedrooms (one of which he was using as his office), a kitchen, bathroom and living room, the flat was worth just over £800,000, thanks to the insane London property prices. He'd paid off the mortgage a couple of years ago, so together with the cash he had stashed away in various investment accounts, he was easily a millionaire. Not bad for an ex-cop in his forties.

He read through the five Word documents, one for each of the compromised ministers, on his laptop a final time before printing them. He then put each print-out in a separate envelope together with the evidence he had uncovered. This included emails, photographs, sworn testimony, and flash drives containing videos and taped transcripts.

When done, he texted Madden to arrange a meeting. Hayes had a feeling the man was going to be extremely satisfied with what he had to show him. Effectively, he was handing him something very close to control of the British Government, and he was expecting something very good in return.

It was 6.30pm and Polly Santana was saying goodbye to one of her clients. Standing on the front doorstep, she watched as the rather stout lady, Middle Eastern and in her late forties, climbed into the chauffeured Rolls Royce that had glided into view from nowhere. As the car moved off, she waved but the woman just turned away. It had been their first session and Polly had found it hard going. The woman had been rather aloof and uncommunicative, and Polly had got the feeling she was just going through the motions and didn't really want to be there. Her husband was probably losing interest in her and looking elsewhere. It was not uncommon in that part of the world where women were seen as a commodity as much as anything else.

Shrugging, she turned and went back inside – it wasn't her problem. She doubted she would see the woman again. Putting her quickly out of mind, she re-entered the small but well-equipped gymnasium built onto the back of the house and busied herself tidying it up. As she did so, her mind was on her next client, Dominic Madden.

He was due in half an hour, assuming he turned up on time that was – he frequently didn't!

Polly always enjoyed the sessions with Madden and looked forward to them. The actual workouts were often more of a sideshow as he would spend more time talking than he did exercising. And while she had no real interest in politics, his usual subject of choice, Polly couldn't help but be intrigued by the stories he told her about the country's politicians and top civil servants, many of them household names. If only half what he told her regarding the machinations, subterfuge and criminality these people got up to was true, the Establishment would have been held in even lower esteem than it already was.

Today, though, Polly had another reason to anticipate their weekly session. She was after information regarding Jack Hayes and figured Dominic Madden was her best chance of getting it. Despite having given a lot of thought as to the best way of doing it, however, she was still unsure. Her initial plan had been to use the tried and tested seduction routine to put him off his guard. On second thoughts though, she had decided he was too canny an operator to fall for something as obvious as that, particularly as she had never shown any interest in him before. If she suddenly started coming on to him, his first thought would be 'why?' and his second thought 'why now?' He'd be on his guard immediately.

Deciding the place was tidy enough for Madden – he never took any notice anyway – Polly went into the kitchen, poured herself a glass of wine and sat down to wait for him. A lot would depend, she knew, on his frame of mind. He was always a lot more talkative and animated when he'd had a frustrating day at the office.

At 7.30 precisely, the doorbell rang. Polly cursed; they were off to a bad start already. Madden was only ever on time when he'd had a good day. His cheerful demeanour when she opened the front door confirmed it.

'Hi Pol,' he grinned cheerfully. 'What tortures have you got lined up for me tonight?'

'You are joking. I'm the one who has to suffer the torture of listening to your rantings and ravings.'

He chuckled, 'Yeah, I know I can be a pain in the arse sometimes. Not to worry though; tonight I'm really up for it.'

'That'll make a nice change,' she replied, a touch acidly.

For the next forty-five minutes, she put him through his paces. The exercise plan she had devised for him was a complete body workout that included running, skipping, weights, stretching exercises and core exercises. To her surprise, for the first time, he actually managed to complete it without stopping once for a rest or to sound off about something. He was struggling at the end though.

'Fucking hell woman, you're supposed to be getting me fit, not killing me,' he gasped.

Surveying him as he stood there panting and dripping with sweat, Polly laughed, 'I'm beginning to think there's more to you than meets the eye. I didn't think you were capable of doing it.'

'Nor did I to be honest.' He sounded surprised at himself.

'Just goes to show what you can achieve when you don't piss about like you usually do,' she said tartly.

Ten minutes later, a freshly showered Madden strolled into Polly's living room and plonked himself down in the armchair opposite her. Picking up the glass of chilled white wine from the coffee table, he took a thirsty gulp.

Although he was only paying Polly for the forty-five-minute session, she was quite happy to chat with him afterwards in her own time, given he was such an intriguing character.

They started off with some general conversation. Topics discussed included the weather, the forest fires in the Amazon, climate change – Madden thought the potential effects were vastly overstated and had doubts whether mankind was even responsible for it. In his view, it was just as likely to be due to some cosmic event in outer space.

Half an hour slipped by quickly and it wasn't long after Polly opened the second bottle that he began to hit his stride. It was, she judged, time to start steering the conversation.

'So, Dominic, how come you're so happy today? One of your little schemes paying off? Whatever it was you were plotting in the pub the other day perhaps? And who, by the way, was that rather dishy hunk you were talking with? The one with the beard.'

Madden narrowed his eyes at her. 'You keep your claws out of him. He's doing some very important work for me at the moment and I don't need you causing any distractions.'

Polly topped up Madden's glass. As she did so, she asked casually, 'Oh really. What's he doing for you?' She did her best to sound as if she wasn't really that interested.

'He's a private investigator. When I need info about someone, he's the man who gets it for me. Very good at it he is too.'

'Well, I wouldn't mind seeing what else he's good at! He's just the type I go for.'

Madden frowned. He was just about to say something when Polly laughed. 'Relax idiot, I'm winding you up. To tell you the truth, I hate men with beards – nasty scratchy things. None too clean either, most of them, I shouldn't wonder.'

From the look on his face, he was clearly unsure as to whether to take her seriously.

'So why *are* you so happy?' she prompted again. 'You're a miserable bastard most of the time.'

If he was offended, he didn't show it. 'Well today I've learned something that could, quite literally, change the balance of power in this country. Who wouldn't be happy?'

'Wow. Whatever it is, it must be startling.' There was a slightly mocking edge to her voice.

Madden smiled. 'Actually, it's not. It's what I can do with the information that's startling. What I can achieve with it.'

'Dominic,' she chided. 'Sometimes I think you're a little boy in a man's body. What planet are you on? You're not even an MP for Christ's sake. How the hell can you change the balance of power?'

For all she knew he probably could, but Polly's intention was to goad him so he would open up. He did have a tendency to boast. When Madden had achieved something, he liked people to know about it.

He frowned. 'Listen, I don't need to be a fucking MP, not even a Cabinet minister for that matter. I've already got more clout than any of them. And with what I've learned today, I will very soon be able to tell the fucking lot of them what to do and there won't be a thing they can do about it.' There was triumph in his voice as he spoke the last sentence. 'And that means the balance of power in this country will lie squarely in these two hands.' He held both his hands out as if to emphasise the point.

Polly eyed him uncertainly as though wondering if he was serious before bursting into derisive laughter. 'Dominic, there've been times when I've wondered if you're the full ticket. Now I know for sure. You're certifiable! You poor thing.' She shook her head pityingly.

He laughed. 'Okay, well maybe not all of them. Not yet at any rate; I'm still working on that. But be in no doubt that I've now got a sizeable chunk of the Cabinet on my side. Some because they want to be – they agree with what I'm trying to achieve – and some because I've left them no choice. If they don't do what I tell them, they'll be out of a job and even quite possibly find themselves before a judge.'

Polly nodded, as if taking him more seriously now. 'I get it. You're telling me that you have stuff on them that is either incriminating or embarrassing. Stuff they wouldn't want making public.'

Madden nodded. 'That's about the size of it. And before you sound off about ethics and all that shit, just remember it's the way politics works – dog eat dog. And it's the politicians that made it that way.'

'For God's sake; you're all as bad as each other.' There was an almost despairing note in her voice.

He shrugged. 'I'm just playing them at their own nasty game. Ethics, I'm afraid, have no place in it.'

'So, I assume you've gone looking for all this "stuff". I mean, it hasn't just dropped into your lap has it?'

'No, not me personally. There are people who specialise in that sort of thing. If there's something to find, they'll find it. For the right price of course.'

And there it was. Suddenly the connection was obvious. Jack Hayes, a policeman, or probably now an ex-policeman, she'd seen deep in conversation with Madden in the pub had to be the private investigator he was talking about. Hiding her elation, Polly asked, 'So, what if your man can't find anything on someone? Not everyone's bent you know.'

He shrugged. 'If it's really necessary, we plant something on them. "Fit them up" I think is the phrase. Today's digital world makes it easy. Anything can be put on someone's computer: pornography, incriminating emails, embarrassing browsing history – take your pick.'

'You do realise there are laws against that sort of thing?'

'Doesn't matter. Most officials, policemen, even judges, can be persuaded to look the other way if they're offered enough. Like I said, ethics are irrelevant. Money is power and power is money – there's nothing else really in politics.'

'And this private investigator of yours is actually prepared to do that? Fit people up!'

Madden didn't reply but the world-weary look on his face was answer enough.

Polly shook her head. 'You live in a different world to me Dominic,' she sighed, doing her best to sound sad and disillusioned. Inside though, she was anything but. After all these years, it looked as though she now had something on Jack Hayes. Something she could use to get revenge for the brutal way he had jilted her.

John Meacher was busy, busier than he'd ever been. On taking over as minister for Media and Communications, he'd hit the ground running. He'd spent the first couple of weeks taking stock of what he'd inherited and had quickly realised just how badly the department had been run under his predecessor. Like most ministers, he had little technical knowledge of his brief and so had to rely on advisors who did. This was the first problem he'd found: the Ministry for Media and Communications had far too many of them; most not fit for purpose. The advice they gave him was often wrong or contradictory, and it didn't take him long to realise he simply couldn't place any credence on what they told him. Which meant, of course, that he couldn't do his own job as he would never know what was really going on. The advisors had to go and go they did. Within a month, most had received their cards and almost immediately things began to improve. Meacher's trusty assistant, Tom Guppy, had played a key role in the process. It was he who'd largely sorted out the mess by identifying the advisors surplus to requirements, and recruiting replacements where necessary.

Not only did this mean Meacher could now get a grip on the job with the aid of good briefing, it also fired a warning shot at others. Grown accustomed to an easy life, all of a sudden, they knew they had to improve, and fast. Within a few weeks, the department began to morph into a smooth, efficient operation that worked in the national interest rather than its own.

That achieved, it was then time for Meacher to start putting policies into place. One of the first issues on his to-do list was the lack of fast, reliable broadband in rural areas. Getting it sorted was a sure-fire vote winner. Millions of angry people had been promised action for years but very little had been done. The problem was the telecoms companies, who saw little profit in providing it due to the enormous costs involved in building the necessary infrastructure. Meacher's solution was to simply bypass them and set up a system of public partnerships that could build their own broadband networks. These would be financed by local businesses and inhabitants.

Sitting at his desk one Friday afternoon, he was reading the letter that was about to be sent to the telecoms companies explaining his intentions regarding the provision of broadband, when the door to his office opened and in walked Tom Guppy. 'Here's the report on the BBC you asked for.'

The issue of how the British Broadcasting Corporation was funded was also high on Meacher's list of priorities. Increasingly, the public was questioning whether the corporation's output merited the enormous amount of public money it was being given. The issue had the potential to be another vote winner and Meacher's intention to introduce a subscription model had Dominic Madden's full backing.

Meacher took the report. 'Thanks Tom.' Rifling through it, he stopped at one page. 'Fucking hell, these people pay themselves well, don't they? No wonder they're so terrified at the prospect of their cosy little world being shaken up.'

'It's nice work if you can get it,' Guppy agreed with a wry smile. 'Millionaires, a lot of them. And all at the taxpayers' expense.'

'Well it won't be for much longer, believe me. It's high time the licence fee was abolished and replaced by a subscription model. If Netflix and Amazon Prime can do it, so can the BBC. It'll mean having to compete in the real world instead of having billions handed to them every year, and they'll absolutely hate it, but that's tough. They'll have to learn to live with it.'

He yawned tiredly and tossed the report onto his desk. 'I think I'll call it a day Tom. This can wait until tomorrow.'

Guppy nodded his head in agreement. 'I was thinking boss, we've both been working like dogs recently so why don't we relax a bit. I did promise to show you some clubs I know, do you remember?'

'That's a bloody good idea,' Meacher agreed. 'I can't remember the last time I had a good night out.'

'Great. I've got nothing on tomorrow evening; how

about you?'
   'No, nothing planned.'
   'Okay, shall I pick you up at 8.00?'
   'I'll look forward to it.'

Simon Turner was so fat he could barely fit behind the handlebars of his Motability scooter. Passers-by on the street couldn't help but look at him – some in curiosity, some in sympathy and some in disgust. He didn't care though; he'd given up caring about anything a long time ago.

Stopping at a rundown coffee bar he frequented, Turner eased his enormous bulk though the door and made his way ponderously inside. Ignoring the look of revulsion the girl behind the counter gave him, he ordered a latte and a large plate of fruit scones. Slumping down at a table with a sigh of relief, he began to eat.

The table was dirty with crumbs and spilled coffee from the previous occupant, but he took no notice. Seemingly in a world of his own, he ignored everyone, and everyone ignored him.

An hour, and several lattes and plates of scones, later, he heaved himself to his feet with difficulty and struggled to the door. The assistant was glad to see him go – the spectacle of the grossly obese man shovelling food into that bloated body was quite nauseating.

Wincing from the pain in his swollen lower legs, he clambered onto the scooter and set off back down the street. A short while later, he entered the driveway of his little semi-detached house.

On the other side of the low fence that separated them, his neighbour was busy weeding the flower beds. On sight of Turner, he pulled a face and turned away. Mr Matlock had been friendly when he had first moved in but on finding out about his new neighbour's past, had ostracised him completely. As, indeed, had most people in the street.

Opening the garage door, he pushed the scooter inside with an effort and then locked the door. There had been a time when he could have safely left it outside, but those days were long gone. Now, it would be stolen within hours.

Going inside the house, he made his way slowly down the little hallway that led to the kitchen. On his right was the staircase, on his left the doorway to the living room.

The kitchen was grimy and littered with dirty plates and empty fast food containers. It smelled bad as well; in fact, the entire house smelled bad. He was so used to it though, he didn't even notice any more. Picking up a bottle of vodka and a jumbo-sized bag of crisps, he went back down the hallway to the living room. It was how he spent his afternoons and evenings; staring at the garbage on the TV while gorging on junk food and drinking himself into oblivion.

Pushing the door open, he shuffled inside and put the

crisps and vodka on the little side table by his armchair. He was about to lower himself into the chair when he suddenly became aware of something in the corner of the room to the side of the window. The curtains were drawn – he never opened them, preferring to sit in semi-darkness – so he couldn't make out what it was.

'Is somebody there?' There was a tremor in his voice as he peered nervously across. Then, as his eyes adjusted to the gloom, he could just make out a tall figure standing motionless.

'Who are you?' Turner cried out in fright. 'What are you doing in my house?'

There was no answer. The figure stayed stock still for a few moments before moving slowly forward. Out of the shadows now, Turner could see it was a tall, lean man dressed all in black, his features hidden by a balaclava.

Rooted to the spot, he stared goggle-eyed as the black figure approached and then stopped in front of him. With a feeling of dread, he sensed something terrible was about to happen.

Holding out a dog-eared photograph, the stranger asked, 'Do you remember this boy?'

Trembling, Turner forced himself to look at the picture. It showed a thin faced young lad about ten years of age. It had been a long time ago, but he recognised him at once. It was the little bastard who had tripped him and sent him crashing down the stairs at the Shirley Heights Boys Home all those years ago. Suddenly, he knew what this was about. His past had finally caught up with him.

Nodding, he muttered in a hoarse voice, 'Yes, I remember him.'

'You helped Thomas Morris sexually assault him. Do you remember that?'

'Yes,' Turner whispered.

'He was a vulnerable and defenceless ten year-old boy who had nothing in the world – no parents, no home, no money – nothing. He was placed in your care and, monsters that you were, you abused him.'

The words were spoken quietly but Turner could sense the suppressed fury raging through the man. It was all true and there was nothing he could say. He lowered his eyes and stared wretchedly at the floor.

'I killed Thomas Morris because of what he did to Sam Clark. And now I'm going to kill you.' Reaching inside his jacket, the man produced a bone-handled knife and lunged forward without warning.

Simon Turner screamed.

It was 8.00 to the minute when the doorbell rang. Tom Guppy was dead on time as Meacher knew he would be – it was his way. Pulling on his jacket, he opened the door to see his assistant standing on the doorstep.

'Ready for the best night of your life?'

Meacher laughed. 'It'll have to be bloody good then.'

'It will be, believe me.' Guppy assured him. He was eyeing Meacher's blue jeans, white shirt and tan leather jacket critically. 'Fucking hell, you look like something from the 1970's. You won't pull much where we're going dressed like that. Are you sure you don't want to go back in and put on something decent? Assuming you have something decent that is.'

'Patronising fucker.'

Guppy laughed. He gestured at the waiting taxi. 'Come on then old man. Let's see if you've still got what it takes.'

Settling himself in the black cab, Meacher was anticipating the evening ahead. He'd been in London by himself for over a month now; his wife Angela having refused to leave Ely. Her excuse had been that she knew no-one in the capital and would miss her friends at home. While it was true, it was also true that they had drifted apart over the years. He knew she simply didn't want to come. That being the case, there was nothing to hold him back tonight. So, whatever it brought, he was up for it.

Leaning forward, Guppy said to the driver. 'Gerry's Bar in Dean Street please.'

The man chuckled as he edged out into the traffic. 'Sounds like you're out for a good night then!'

Twenty minutes later, he pulled up outside a row of dilapidated terrace houses dating back to the 1500's. Getting out while Guppy paid the driver, Meacher looked around but there was no sign of a bar. Seeing his puzzlement, the driver pointed at an unmarked wooden door badly in need of a coat of paint. 'It's in there.'

'Come on. You're going to love this place.' Pushing the door open, Guppy lead the way down a rickety wooden staircase that creaked and groaned alarmingly. As they descended into the depths of the ancient building, he muttered in a tone of near reverence, 'It may not look it, but this is one of the oldest and best drinking establishments in the entire city of London.'

The stairs opened out into a large cellar, the ceiling of which was so low that Meacher had to duck under the blackened wooden beams that supported it. Faded pictures and prints adorned the walls, and the dim lighting came from ancient brass lanterns. Wooden tables and chairs were scattered haphazardly, and the perimeter led off into little alcoves where one could sit and see but not be seen. There was absolutely nothing modern in the place – no steel, plastic or glass. It was an authentic, old-fashioned drinking den pure and simple and, as he entered, Meacher felt he was stepping back in time. He'd never seen anything quite like it.

Finding an empty table, they sat down. While Guppy was getting the drinks, Meacher looked around in fascination. The bar was busy but quiet with just a low hum of conversation – no loud music, raucous shouts or peals of laughter to spoil the setting.

They had been putting the world to rights for a while when Guppy drained his glass and said, 'Time for something to eat, I think. There's a very good Thai restaurant not far from here. I can highly recommend it.'

'Sounds good to me.' Much as he was enjoying Gerry's Bar, Meacher was relieved to be going. He'd already had a bit too much to drink and the night was still young. Sadly, the days when he could hold his own in long drinking sessions were behind him. By the time they reached the Thai Cottage Restaurant in D'Arblay Street, he was feeling better thanks to the walk and bracing air. The place looked nothing much from the outside and didn't look much better inside. The food, however, was excellent.

'So, what's this great club you're taking me to then?' With a full stomach, Meacher was ready for the next instalment of the evening's entertainment.

'Well, there's quite a few but most of them aren't really suitable for an old git like you,' Guppy said with an annoying smirk. 'I'd hate to see you making a prat of yourself.'

'Fuck off.'

His companion laughed. 'I think you might just about be able to handle the Hot Banana club though.'

'Sounds interesting.' Meacher was inebriated enough to have temporarily forgotten he was a Cabinet minister and that there were certain types of establishment he shouldn't be seen frequenting. He got to his feet, suddenly keen to see what the intriguingly named club had to offer. 'Come on then. I'll settle the bill.'

On entering, Meacher saw immediately that the Hot Banana Club was aptly named. The ground floor was devoted to a circular pole dancing stage upon which a stripper was, at that moment, engaged in her routine. The stage was surrounded by tables, where customers could sit and watch the performers. The ones nearest the stage were already occupied, so they had no choice but to sit further back, Guppy grumbling, 'Fuck, we're not going to have much of a view from here.'

They could see enough though, and for the next couple of hours, they sat drinking beer while watching a succession of well-endowed women doing their thing. Other women circulated the room touting for business. Meacher couldn't help but notice a steady stream of them leading the punters over to a staircase that led to a lower level.

'They have rooms down there where they do the business.' His companion had seen him looking.

'No! I'd never have guessed.'

Guppy ignored the sarcastic response. 'It can get a bit hectic though, so many of the guys take them home, or

to a hotel if they're married. Why don't you have a go?'
Looking about, Guppy spotted a couple of women about
twenty feet away. 'How about one of those two?'

Clad in low-cut tops and short skirts that left little to
the imagination, the women were chatting idly to each
other. They both looked bored.

'It's tempting, I must admit. It's been a while now.'

'Go for it then. Which one do you fancy – the blonde
with the big knockers or the brunette?'

Meacher surveyed the two women. The brunette was a
bit on the scrawny side for his liking. He preferred
women with meat on their bones and the blonde certainly
had plenty of that. It was a no-brainer really.

'The one with the tits looks good to me.' As he said it,
the blonde noticed him eyeing her. After giggling something to her companion, she came sidling over to where
they stood. Giving Meacher a mischievous smile, she
asked, 'Looking for some action?'

It was a long time since John Meacher had done anything like this and, embarrassingly, he found himself
stuck for something to say. Tom Guppy came to his rescue. Grinning, he said, 'We certainly are.'

The woman chuckled. 'That's great. My name is Irina.
And you?'

'I'm Tom and my friend here is John.'

'Nice to make your acquaintance, both of you.' She
spoke with a slight accent.

'Where are you from Irina?' Meacher tore his gaze away
from her enormous breasts with an effort. They really
were magnificent and with a sudden certainty, he knew

this one would do for him.

'I am from Debrecen in Hungary.' Irina looked from one to the other. 'So, boys, what sort of action are you looking for? A threesome?'

Guppy laughed. 'No, no, count me out. I'm going upstairs in a moment.'

Irina smiled knowingly. 'Yes, there's plenty going on up there.' She looked enquiringly at Meacher. 'Just you and me then?'

Suddenly nervous, he took a deep breath before nodding.

'Good.' She sounded pleased.

Glancing at Guppy, Meacher asked curiously, 'What happens upstairs?'

It was Irina who answered. 'Whatever type of sex you want – gay, lesbian, group, bondage – it's all up there.' She looked at Guppy. 'What are you into?'

He laughed. 'Why don't you come up with me and find out for yourself?'

Irina smiled. 'Maybe next time. Tonight, I am with your friend.' Taking Meacher's arm, she said, 'Let's go.'

'See you tomorrow then boss.' Guppy grinned in that annoying way of his as he watched them walk away.

'So, John. Where do you want to do it – a room here or a hotel? I think a hotel is better. Downstairs is not very nice, too many people.' She wrinkled her nose.

He looked at the staircase leading below; there was a queue backing up the stairs now. It was clearly very busy down there and he didn't find the prospect at all appealing. 'I agree. We'll go to a hotel. Do you know one around here?'

Irina nodded. 'Yes, we can go to the Rathbone. It's just a few minutes' walk. Lots of the girls here use it.'

'Let's get to it then.'

As they exited the club, she slid her arm around his waist and led him away down the street. His attention firmly fixed on his companion, Meacher failed to notice the man sitting in a car across the road, pointing a camera at him.

'Ladies and Gentlemen, your attention please.' Standing on a chair, Dominic Madden waited until the buzz of conversation around the room died down. 'I've invited you all here tonight as both a celebration of what we've achieved and as a well-deserved thank you for all your hard work. This time next week the election will be over and the latest opinion polls show we are on course to win a thumping majority of around 100 seats. Looking at where we were a year ago, I very much doubt any of us here would have believed it possible.' This was greeted with a round of applause.

They were assembled in the Toy Room, a high-class and extremely expensive club in London's Mayfair. It was a popular venue for corporate events and Madden had hired one of its function rooms to throw a celebration party for the forthcoming election victory. Most people would have waited until after the election but as the result was a foregone conclusion, he saw no need to wait. Invited to the party were the Cabinet ministers loyal to Madden and a number of the backroom staff who had played important roles behind the scenes. Conspicuous by their absence were the few remaining ministers who were opposed to Madden and his way of doing things.

It was ten months since the night John Meacher had stumbled out of the Hot Banana Club with a hooker on his arm. For days afterwards, he had lived in dread of the media finding out. As the days passed with no lurid headlines appearing in the papers, it began to look as though he'd got away with it. Resolving "never again" Meacher threw himself into his new job with renewed vigour. Madden, meanwhile, had been wasting no time in getting rid of the deadwood, as he termed it, in the Cabinet.

Once appointed, the new ministers were given clear instructions on what he expected them to do. One of which was that they were all to implement Madden's ruthless approach to management in their own departments. This led, inevitably, to large-scale clear-outs of personnel, major changes in working practices, dumping of existing policies and the introduction of new ones. The Whitehall machine was outraged and fought back in the only way it knew how – with lies, obfuscation, threats, go-slows, walk-outs, legal challenges – all to no avail. In Dominic Madden and his new Cabinet, they came up against an immovable object.

Wide-ranging measures were put in place to cut unnecessary costs wherever possible and release the funds for projects that were more urgent, such as police staffing levels, transport, health, and care for the elderly. One of the first moves to this end was the cutting of the bloated overseas aid budget from a massive fifteen billion pounds annually to five billion. The ten billion saved was immediately put into increasing police numbers in an effort to bring the ever-rising levels of street crime under control.

Madden then launched a nationwide publicity campaign to advertise the new policies being introduced. It was a massive operation that involved the press, TV and social media. Leaflets detailing the Government's plans were delivered to every house and business in the country. He even ordered all Conservative MPs to spend at least one day a week for a month knocking on doors and asking homeowners for their opinions. This was unprecedented – politicians actually *talking* to the people they represented and taking an interest in their views.

It was all anathema to the Establishment and the left-leaning, metropolitan elite who couldn't have cared less about the people. All they could see was the old order that had suited them so well, and for so long, being dismantled before their very eyes. In desperation, they resorted to a Project Fear campaign warning of terrible consequences for the country. Amongst the ludicrous claims made were that the economy would collapse, vital drugs would run short, prices would rocket, even that dead bodies would pile up in the streets. The trouble, however, was that the people had heard it all before. The Establishment had made the same claims during its demented attempts to stop the country leaving the European Union. The public simply didn't believe any of it.

Rather, encouraged by what they were seeing and hearing from the Government, they swung behind it. Within a matter of months, the opinion polls showed the Conservatives were reversing the decline of recent years and were beginning to pull ahead of the opposition. Christmas came and went, and by the time it was announced the General Election would be held on April 30th, they were in an unassailable position.

From the fringes of the crowd, John Meacher watched as Dominic Madden lapped up the applause. Standing next to him, Jack Hayes shook his head in wonder. 'You have to hand it to him John. I still think he's got a loose screw rattling around in his head somewhere but what he's achieved is incredible. Without him, we'd be looking at five years of Marxist mayhem Venezuela style.'

Meacher nodded in agreement. 'I know. I can hardly believe it myself. Say what you like about the man, and many people have, myself included, but he gets things done.'

Hayes drank from his glass. Looking around the room, his gaze fell on Gavin Osbourne who was at that moment trying unsuccessfully to get Dominic Madden's attention. He got the impression that Madden was deliberately ignoring the man.

'He can be a rude bastard though, can't he? Look at that, Osbourne's trying to say something to him and he's taking absolutely no notice.'

Meacher followed Hayes's gaze. 'He does that all the time with Osbourne; treats him like an idiot. I don't know why the man puts up with it.'

'Well let's face it, he is a bit of an idiot. Nice enough chap but he's really not Prime Minister material, is he?'

'No, he's not. Never will be either.'

'So why *is* he still Prime Minister?' There was puzzlement in Hayes's voice. 'I mean, Madden has put go-getters in charge of nearly all the ministries but left a dumb fucker in the most important job of all. It doesn't make any sense.'

'He won't be there much longer.'

Hayes looked keenly at Meacher. 'Oh really.'

'The reason Madden's tolerated Osbourne until now is that for all his faults, the public perception of him is that he's a decent man. They are also familiar with him, something that can't be said for most of the Cabinet who haven't been in their posts for long. For that reason, Madden has seen him as an electoral asset to be used. However, now that the election is all but over, so, I'm afraid, is Osbourne. His usefulness has come to an end. This time next week, the country will have a new Prime Minister. Osbourne will be history.'

Hayes whistled. 'Does the poor bastard know yet?'

'Yes, of course he does – it's all been planned. The day after the election, Osbourne will announce he is retiring with immediate effect due to an ongoing health issue. He'll say he would have gone earlier but only stayed to help deliver the election victory.'

'And how does he feel about it? I mean, is he going willingly or is he being forced out?'

Meacher snorted, 'Well, what do you think? He's absolutely livid and who can blame him. Madden's given him an ultimatum though. Resign and keep your dignity or be forced out by a Cabinet vote of no-confidence. He doesn't want the humiliation that will bring, so he has no option but to go.'

'Which raises the million-dollar question – who is going to replace him?' Hayes looked at Meacher keenly.

'I am,' was the matter-of-fact reply. 'Madden's asked me to do it and I've said yes. The other Cabinet members have been informed and enough of them are happy with it to make it happen.'

Hayes nodded. 'Yeah, you said a while back he was planning on making you Prime Minister. I just hope you know what you're doing though. The second you've out-lived your usefulness; he'll shaft you just like all the others.'

Meacher smiled grimly. 'He can try. He'll find I don't go as easily.'

'Well, if you need my help, just ask. I never have liked the arrogant bastard.'

'Thanks, but it's all in hand.' Just at that moment there was a sudden clatter of drums and twanging of electric guitars. Looking over, the two men could see a band had appeared on a small stage at the end of the room and were warming up. The party was about to get going.

Wincing at the discordant racket, Meacher leaned his head towards Hayes. 'What about you Jack? What are you going to do now? With the election in the bag, Madden doesn't need you anymore either.'

'I've already terminated our "agreement". As you say, he doesn't need me now and I certainly don't need him. I don't mind telling you John, I've made a packet out of this. The man's got very deep pockets.'

'The men *he's* working for have very deep pockets don't you mean?'

Hayes shrugged. 'All the same to me. To answer your question, I'm emigrating to sunnier climes – the Caribbean's looking favourite at the moment.'

'Fuck, he *has* been paying you well,' Meacher chuckled. 'Sun, sea, sand and women in skimpy bikinis. What more could a man want?'

Hayes smiled. 'Yeah, all that.' He added more seriously, 'It's not enough though; I need to be beyond the reach of the British security forces. It has to be a country that doesn't have an extradition treaty with the UK. Madden may have paid me well but I've earned every penny, believe me. I've pulled some stunts for him that could have me banged up for years. Blackmail, framing, intimidation – you wouldn't believe it if I told you.'

'Knowing our friend, I certainly can believe it.'

Hayes continued, 'I've seriously pissed off some powerful people and they will come looking for me. I don't intend to be around when they do.' He drained his glass and handed it to a passing waiter. 'Well enjoy the party John, I'm off. I've got better things to do than get drunk and listen to self-congratulatory speeches.'

Meacher chuckled. 'What's her name?'

Hayes grinned. 'You know me too well! Ludmilla. She's Russian. She could be joining me in the Caribbean if she plays her cards right.'

Meacher smiled. 'Enjoy your retirement. I'll miss you – I think.'

'We've both got what we wanted John. You've got

power and everything that brings, and I've got all the money I'll ever need. Watch out for that mad fucker Madden though. Don't underestimate him.' Hayes clapped Meacher on the shoulder and left the room.

Little did either know their worlds were about to come crashing down.

For John Meacher, it started five weeks later. The election had been duly won, Gavin Osbourne had resigned, and Meacher had been voted in by the Cabinet as his replacement. All as per the script laid out by the puppet master, Dominic Madden.

On only his third day in the job, he had just sat down to begin work on a large pile of papers when his office door was suddenly thrown open and in stormed a grim-faced Madden. Throwing a newspaper on the desk, he snarled, 'What the fuck is this?'

It was a copy of the Guardian and the frontpage headline read: 'Prime Minister in LGBT bias storm'. This was followed by a photograph showing an extract from a Twitter thread that was signed by a John Meacher MP/Ely. The date on the tweet showed it had been posted two years previously and was in reply to someone complaining about society's supposedly hostile attitude to transgender people.

The tweet read: 'Sorry but you have to accept biological facts. Humans can't alter their sex – end of. Having his penis removed and an artificial vagina constructed does not turn a man into a woman – he's just a man with a fake vagina. This whole transgender business is utter rubbish. And don't try and shout me down just because you don't like what I'm saying. I have the right to state my views just as you do yours.'

The article went on to say that the Twittersphere was alive with outrage over the Prime Minister's "incendiary comments".

Meacher looked up at the glowering Madden with astonishment. 'I didn't write this. I don't even have a Twitter account for Christ's sake.'

'It's apparently signed by you and it's been verified as having been posted from a computer in your Ely office. I've sent someone up there to check it out.' Aware of Meacher's ignorance of all things digital, he added impatiently, 'It's all to do with MAC and IP addresses – digital signposts, if you like, that enable Internet activity to be tracked. This particular piece of Internet activity is pointing directly to you!' His tone was accusatory.

Meacher glared at him, not attempting to hide his irritation. While he was well aware that he owed his job to Madden, he had no intention of letting the man treat him in the same dismissive manner as he had his predecessor.

'I don't give a fuck. It wasn't me. I'm not the only person in that office you know. It could have been posted by any number of people.'

'Well, we'll know more when my man reports back.' Madden muttered, clearly still unhappy. He sounded less confrontational though.

Picking up the newspaper, Meacher read the article again. 'If this was posted two years ago, why is it only now causing a fuss? Why not at the time?'

Madden shook his head as though talking to a moron. 'Because two years ago you were just a provincial MP. But now, you're Prime Minister of the United Kingdom and so the media, and anyone else with an axe to grind, will be looking everywhere they can think of to try and find something bad about you.' He jabbed a finger at the offending article. 'And it looks as if they may have succeeded, doesn't it?'

'Whoever has written this is quite right though, aren't they? And even if they weren't, why on earth are people getting so steamed up? It's not accusatory or insulting in any way.' Meacher sighed wearily. 'It really is complete bollocks.'

'Of course it is but that isn't the issue here. Whether we agree with them or not, the fact is an awful lot of people are taking this "bollocks" seriously, and social media gives them a voice. It doesn't put you in a good light, particularly as it comes right at the beginning of your premiership. We could have done without it.'

Meacher shrugged. 'I'll deny it of course.'

'Obviously. That's the first thing.' Lighting a cigarette, Madden started pacing up and down, his bony brow furrowed in concentration. 'But we'll need to do more. We need to get something out there, some announcement or other, to divert attention away from this. Then we have to find out who the hell *is* responsible and make sure it doesn't happen again. I accept it wasn't you – you're not that stupid, not quite!' There was the flicker of a smile on his face as he said it.

'Ha ha.' Meacher showed Madden his middle finger.

'Your man Tom Guppy might be able to shed some light on the matter. Get hold of him and see if he knows anything.' Muttering, 'I'll talk to you later,' Madden left the office. He was clearly unhappy with the turn of events. Meacher wasn't too happy himself.

He hit the intercom button. 'Tom, I need to see you.' To his surprise, there was no response. He tried again with the same result. Getting to his feet, he walked down the corridor to his assistant's office. It was empty. Going back to his own office, he called Security and was told that Guppy hadn't been in for a couple of days. Puzzled now because his assistant wasn't the type to go missing without notice, he tried his phone but it just rang and rang. All he could do was leave a message.

That done, he rather glumly turned his attention back to the pile of papers on his desk. It was far from an ideal start but there was nothing he could do about it. As the government's political fixer, this was one for Dominic Madden to sort out.

It was a warm, sunny afternoon, and Polly Santana was sitting alone at a table outside the Highwayman, a small pub in London's East End. Inside, it was a grotty little place with surly, unhelpful staff but it did have the redeeming feature of a lovely terrace garden. She liked to sit there on a nice day and read her emails, browse the Internet and just sit and watch people go by. It was quiet and relaxing.

Today, however, she had more on her mind than emails. Polly Santana was frustrated, and in more ways than one. Her first problem was sex, or rather lack of it! It had been several weeks since she'd last had a man and, being the highly sexed woman she was, she wasn't going to be able to do without for much longer.

Her second issue was Jack Hayes. It had been over six months since Dominic Madden had let slip the man was engaging in illegal activity with the clear intention of incriminating Government ministers, and she still hadn't done anything with the information. It had been a very busy time for her, what with her ailing mother needing daily care and frequent hospital visits. The burden had finally been lifted three weeks previously when the old lady had passed away.

Now it was time to get on with it. What she couldn't figure out was how to best use the information. One option was to take it to the police but she could just imagine their reaction:

'And where did you get this information Madam?'

'Dominic Madden; you don't say!'

'Will he verify it?'

'Why are you coming forward now, six months later?'

They would have a good laugh and tell her to stop wasting police time. It was a clear non-starter. There had to be another way.

After grappling with it for a while and getting nowhere, Polly's thoughts switched to her need for a man. Much as the prospect of getting even with Jack Hayes appealed, this was more urgent. Seeking inspiration, she picked up her phone and started flicking through her list of contacts. There were dozens as she rarely, if ever, deleted any. Suddenly a name from the past flashed into view – an ex-lover from a couple of years ago. Matt Stevens had been a Detective Sergeant in the Metropolitan Police and the thought suddenly struck her that he could be the answer to both her problems.

Calling as much in hope than anything else, her spirits lifted as a deep growl answered, 'Matt Stevens.'

'Hi Matt, it's Polly.'

There was a short pause and then, 'Polly who?'

She laughed. 'Don't give me that, you know perfectly

well.'

She could almost see the grin splitting his bearded face as he replied, 'It's been a while Polly. Are you calling to report a crime?' There was humour in the gruff voice.

'Well, actually I am. I wonder if we could meet up somewhere so I can tell you about it. There's something else as well.'

'What's wrong with the nearest police station then?'

'Be a waste of time Matt, they won't take me seriously. This is something the average copper couldn't handle.'

'I'm an average copper.'

Polly giggled. 'I don't remember you being average; quite the opposite actually.'

'Well, you do have a way of, how shall I put it, spurring a man on. Is this perhaps the other thing you mentioned?'

She chuckled. 'We're getting ahead of ourselves. I know you will at least listen to what I have to say. Having heard it, I'm hoping you will then take it further. I'm not wasting your time Matt, this is something big, believe me. So, is there any chance of us meeting up?'

There was a pause at the other end as though he was thinking. Then, 'OK, how about this evening?'

'You're a darling. My place or yours?'

'It'll have to be yours. My other half would claw you to shreds.'

'See you later then. I hope you're still as I remember you.'

In the end, Jack Hayes was extremely unlucky. If the police had arrived half an hour later, he would have been gone, safely on his way to the airport. All they would have found was an empty flat. Unfortunately for him, however, the chain of events initiated by Polly Santana's conversation with her policeman ex-boyfriend had moved with lightning speed once the ramifications were realised.

As a result, even though Hayes, having decided it was time to vacate UK shores, had wasted no time, he was just too late. Booked on the overnight flight from Gatwick to Michael Manley International Airport in Kingston, Jamaica, he was taking a shower while waiting for the taxi when he was suddenly aware of a loud banging on the front door.

Assuming the taxi firm had got the time wrong, he swore irritably. 'For fucks sake.' Wrapping a towel round his lower half, he stepped out of the shower and hurried to the door.

Standing on the doorstep was a tall thin man dressed in plain clothes. Behind him were two policemen, one of them obviously homosexual from the way his eyes latched onto Hayes's well-muscled torso. Looking beyond them, Hayes could see a police car parked across his driveway blocking any attempt at escape.

'Yes?' Outwardly calm and collected, no one would have suspected that alarm bells were going off like a siren in his head.

The thin man flashed an ID badge. 'Inspector Paul Cooper of the Metropolitan Police. Are you Jack Hayes?'

'Yes officer, I am. What can I do for you?'

'I have a warrant for your arrest.'

'On what charge?'

'Perverting the course of justice will do for starters. We'll discuss it all back at the station.'

Hayes was thunderstruck. Literally on the point of leaving and he'd been nabbed! Shaking his head in disbelief, he muttered, 'I'll get dressed.'

'Go with him Parker and see he doesn't try and do a runner.' Noticing the look on the gay policeman's face as he stepped forward, he added dryly, 'On second thoughts, it'll probably be safer for our friend if you do it Brown.'

Ten minutes later, Hayes had been arrested, read his rights, bundled into the back of the police car and was on his way to South Lewisham Police Station.

Jack Hayes wasn't the only one feeling the heat. Holed up in the Prime Minister' apartment at No 10, John Meacher was an increasingly worried man.

The media-driven frenzy over his supposed tweet the week before had begun dying out, thanks largely to other events having taken over the news. One was the recent dreadful weather which had caused flooding in many areas, and another was the furore over who was to pay for the Duke and Duchess of Sussex's security arrangements. The couple, having stated they no longer wished to serve in a royal capacity, had made it a contentious issue with the public. Most people could see no good reason why they should pay for the security of the already over-privileged pair if they weren't prepared to work on behalf of the country.

Spotting a heaven-sent opportunity to divert attention away from the Twitter affair, Dominic Madden had immediately seen to it that a number of contradictory statements were put out with the intention of sowing confusion, and so stoking the issue. It worked a treat and the press's obsession with all things royal had seen it quickly relegate the Twitter affair to minor news.

With great relief, Meacher was just turning his attention back to affairs of state when news broke that Madden's attack dog, Jack Hayes, had been arrested and charged with a number of offenses. Given the man's deep involvement in Madden's takeover of the UK Cabinet, this had the potential to blow the whole thing apart. It was a serious development.

The very next day, to his absolute disbelief, he found himself headlining in the newspapers again. One screamed: 'Prime Minister seen leaving sex club in the early hours.' Another raged: 'Is this any way for the Prime Minister of the UK to behave?'

The follow-up articles all showed the same picture of Meacher leaving the Hot Banana Club with his arm around a tarty looking woman and another of them entering a hotel apparently some time later. While the articles were thankfully short on detail, the newspapers had clearly done their homework on the two establishments and made great play of the fact that one was a high-class strip club cum brothel, and the other a rather seedy establishment used by whores to entertain their clients.

The story was quickly taken up by the TV and radio stations and it wasn't long before No 10 was being pressured for a response to the articles. Dominic Madden would normally have been the man to handle it but he happened to be away in Italy taking part in a seminar. Thus, it was up to Meacher to deal with the fallout. As a holding measure to keep the media at bay temporarily, he instructed the Downing Street press office to say he would be putting out a statement the following day.

That gave him less than twenty-four hours. As he mulled the situation over, he realised with a growing sense of panic that, thanks to the photo, the story was undeniable. He'd been caught with his trousers down – almost literally.

More seriously, his behaviour could be construed as a breach of the Ministerial Code; a set of rules and principles that outlines the expected standards of conduct for UK ministers. It was inevitable that their numerous enemies in the media and Whitehall would use this to try and force him out. The saving grace was that the code was not legally enforceable, so there was a slim chance he might be able to hang in there long enough to let the storm blow over. It was a long shot, given the enmity he and Madden were facing, but it was his only hope. Whatever happened though, he wasn't going to make it easy for the bastards by resigning. If they wanted his scalp, they were going to have to work for it.

He was going to have to admit, in public, that the story was true and apologise unreservedly. For someone just elected to the highest office in the land, this was going to be an excruciating thing to have to do with the whole world looking on. He would be a laughingstock and he knew it. Shaking his head in near despair at the prospect, blind fury suddenly welled up inside him. How the fuck had this happened? There had obviously been more people involved in their night out the previous year than just himself and Tom Guppy. Someone had followed them with the intention of catching him in a compromising situation. The why was obvious; what wasn't so obvious was who? Was it Tom Guppy? The night out had been his suggestion but Meacher dismissed the thought immediately. There was simply no reason for his assistant to be behind it. No, he mused, it had to be someone else.

Thinking of Guppy, Meacher was about to buzz his assistant before remembering he was still AWOL. With all the goings-on, he had completely forgotten. It had been over a week now since anyone had seen him. Meacher couldn't help but wonder if his disappearance was connected in any way to the press stories and the arrest of Jack Hayes. He was beginning to suspect the flurry of setbacks in recent days were more than just coincidence. Something was going on.

Pouring a large glass of whisky to settle himself, he sat down to compose the public statement he was going to have to read out the following day. As he did so, an uncomfortable feeling that there was more to come filled him with foreboding.

For a predatory pike, it was about as perfect a hunting spot as could be found. Situated on a sharp bend of the river that slowed the rush of water to a gentle stream, the slack water on the outer curve was deep and thickly populated with reed beds. Trees overhung the water, providing the pike with both shade and protection from birds of prey and other threats. All-in-all, it was the ideal ambush point for the fish to pick off passing prey struggling in the more turbulent inner channel.

Which, of course, made it the perfect spot for the keen pike fisherman. And the man on the bank was a very keen fisherman. Pike were his favourite – the struggle they put up was unmatched by any other freshwater fish. But he also enjoyed fishing for other large river fish, such as trout and carp.

Comfortably seated on a fold-up canvas chair, thermos flask of hot tea on the bank by his side, he was the picture of contentment. And with good reason. It was a lovely afternoon and the sun was shining – the peace and quiet broken only by birds twittering in the trees. It was a magical spot and one he frequented regularly.

Given the time of year, he wasn't expecting to catch any pike as they were a winter fish. So, when the float suddenly started bobbing and then disappeared underwater, he assumed it would be something else. As soon as he struck though and felt the strength of the creature on the end of the line, he knew it was a pike, and a big one at that. Playing the fish, he let it exhaust itself before reeling it in a few minutes later.

About two feet long, it was a good specimen although nothing spectacular – he had caught many bigger over the years. His record catch was twice as big, caught a couple of years ago at this same spot. As the pike thrashed feebly on the bank, he took a moment to admire the sleek, elongated body that could propel it forward like a torpedo, and the large, powerful jaws lined with hundreds of needle-sharp teeth. Olive-green colouring on the back and sides was perfect camouflage for lurking unseen in river vegetation. All-in-all, the pike was one of nature's most efficient hunting machines, equipped to catch and eat virtually anything the rivers could offer. Other fish, frogs, snakes, insects, and even small water birds didn't have a chance against it.

Careful to keep his fingers away from the wicked teeth, he removed the hook before returning the fish to the water. Laying his rod down on the bank, the fisherman decided to call it a day. He already had a fat trout he'd caught earlier which would do nicely for his dinner that evening. Picking up the thermos flask, he poured the last of the tea into a mug, rolled a cigarette and sat there gazing out over the river while he smoked it.

Ten minutes later, he was about to flick the butt into the water and get on his way when something to the left caught his eye. Hovering motionless over the water, no more than three metres away, was a dragonfly. A male, from its vivid blue, purple and green iridescent colouring – females were usually a less striking brownish colour – its attention was fixed on something on the surface.

Sitting back again, the fisherman watched with interest as the insect went about its business. A keen student of the river's environment, he knew he was looking at another of nature's most effective predators. For smaller insects and bugs, the dragonfly was a terrifying enemy with a ninety-five percent kill rate when hunting.

One reason for its prowess was its amazing flying ability, courtesy of two sets of wings on each side. These allowed it to fly in any direction, including backwards, and hover motionless for a minute or more. Another was its near 360-degree vision, with just one blind spot directly behind. Once a dragonfly had spotted its prey, it never lost sight of it. And, as if all that wasn't enough, it was equipped with two fearsome mandibles, complete with sharp serrated edges that acted as teeth. These enabled it to catch, kill and eat prey, all while still in motion. Just as with the pike, the dragonfly was a truly fearsome creature.

He watched it buzz around busily for a couple of minutes before vanishing as quickly as it had appeared. Packing up his gear, he made his way up the bank, through the wooded area behind, and then began the long trudge home. Forty minutes later he reached the top of the low hill that led down to the cottage where he lived. As he descended, the man was whistling cheerfully – it had been a pleasant and relaxing day. He was thinking about the delicious dinner of pan-fried trout he was going to have later when he noticed the strange vehicle parked in the driveway. Frowning, he came to an abrupt halt. He didn't get many visitors. Looking around, he couldn't see anything untoward; everything seemed normal. Except it wasn't! There was someone here; someone who shouldn't be.

He called out, 'Hello.'

There was no answer. After another look around, he advanced slowly towards the front door. It was unlocked and he knew immediately his visitor, whoever it was, was in the house. A sick feeling rose in his stomach as it suddenly dawned on him what this was probably all about. Stepping inside warily, he saw the living room door was ajar. It had been shut when he'd gone out. Going in, he came face-to-face with his uninvited guest. It was the same man – the one from five years ago.

There were no preliminaries. The man's voice was cold, his manner perfunctory. 'It's time. Pack a bag; we're leaving in ten minutes.'

Ron Collins nodded gloomily. He was dreading what was to come but knew he had no choice.

Screwing up yet another sheet of paper in frustration, John Meacher dropped it in the rapidly filling waste bin. Composing the statement he was going to have to release the next day was proving difficult.

He knew what he wanted to say, that was easy. The difficult bit was finding the right words. His statement was going to have to be apologetic in tone but not craven. It needed to suggest he had no intention of resigning, but without actually saying so. He didn't want to look weak but nor could he risk appearing arrogant. He was also wondering if an element of humour mightn't be incorporated into it – the old "boys will be boys" type of thing. It would play well with some but outrage others. The idea appealed to him. No matter how many times he tried though, Meacher couldn't get it right. The written word just wasn't his forte.

Pouring the last of the whisky into the tumbler, he wondered, yet again, where the hell his assistant had got to. This was the sort of thing Tom Guppy was paid to do.

Drowsiness creeping up on him, Meacher leaned back in his chair and closed his eyes wearily. He had drunk too much whisky and it had been a long, eventful day. Muttering a heartfelt 'fuck them all' he let his mind go blank and drifted off into an uneasy sleep.

It was a short-lived respite though. Just twenty minutes later, the insistent ringing of his phone jolted him back to the present. Fumbling on the desk for the damn thing, he saw with great relief it was none other than his missing assistant.

'Where the hell have you been Tom? I've been worried. You haven't been answering your phone, I've left messages which you haven't answered. What on earth is going on?'

Guppy ignored the questions. 'We need to meet boss.'

Irritated by his tone, Meacher was about to let rip when he thought better of it. At least his assistant was back on the scene and, given what was going on, his presence was badly needed.

'All right, come round now. You have some explaining to do,' he growled testily.

'I can't. You'll have to come to my place.'

Unable to hide his annoyance now, Meacher snapped, 'Listen, I'm running things, not you. I don't know where the fuck you've been the last few days, but all hell's been let loose here. I assume you do know about it?' There was sarcasm in his voice as he spoke the last sentence.

'Yes, of course I do. That's what I need to see you about. But you'll have to come to my place.' Guppy was insistent.

'Why for Christ's sake?'

'Because what I have to tell you is for your ears only. It has to be here where I can be sure we won't be overheard.'

Meacher let out an exasperated sigh. 'Okay, I'll come over now. But I'm warning you Tom, this better be good.'

'I very much doubt you'll think it good,' Guppy said in a strange voice. With that, he ended the call.

Frowning, Meacher muttered, 'For fucks sake, what now!' Crossing over to the window, he looked down at the entrance to No 10. All day long the street outside had been a scrum of reporters and cameramen clamouring to hear the government's response to the newspaper articles. Despite being told on three separate occasions there would be no statement that day, they had refused to move, firing questions at everyone who went in and out of the building.

Now, finally, at 6.00 in the evening they had all packed up and gone home. At least he would be spared having to dodge the inevitable barrage of shouted questions.

The traffic having eased, it took Meacher's security team no more than fifteen minutes to drive him to Ackerman Street where Tom Guppy lived. He would have much preferred to go by himself but, as Prime Minister, he had to be escorted everywhere.

'Wait here for me,' he said, getting out of the car. His mood, already sour given the day's events, hadn't been improved by the way he had been summoned. That said, he was curious as to what his assistant had been up to. It should be an interesting conversation, he was thinking as he went up the steps. Little did he know just how interesting it would turn out to be.

When the front door opened, Meacher was struck immediately by the noticeable lack of warmth with which Guppy received him. He made no comment though – maybe they were just both in a bad mood!

Once inside, he wasted no time on the preliminaries. 'Right Tom, why have you dragged me here? What the hell's going on?'

'By "what's going on" I assume you mean the Twitter and sex club articles in the papers, the fact that Jack Hayes has been arrested, and everything turning to shit in your first week as PM.' There was a slightly mocking note in Guppy's voice.

'Yes, and the fact you've been missing for the last week. Where have you been?'

Guppy shrugged. 'I've had some business that needing attending to.' He didn't elaborate nor did he sound apologetic.

Meacher narrowed his eyes in puzzlement. This was a different Tom Guppy to the one he was used to. There was a coolness in his manner he hadn't seen before. The employer/employee dynamic was gone.

'You can't just take off like ...'

'And with regard to the newspaper articles,' Guppy continued as if he hadn't heard, 'I was responsible for those.' Walking over to the sideboard, he poured himself a drink. 'I suggest you have one as well; you're going to need it.' His face was stony as he spoke the words.

'What do you mean you were responsible for the articles? I don't understand.'

'Exactly what I say. I used your computer in the Ely office to publish the tweet and I arranged for a photographer to follow us on our lad's night out last year. That's where the pictures in the newspapers came from. I set you up.'

John Meacher was having trouble taking it in. First the tweet, then the sex club scandal and now this. The person he trusted more than anyone else claiming he was behind it all. And then there was his manner – previously always friendly and humorous but now cold; hostile even.

Staring at Guppy in amazement, all he could manage was a spluttered, 'Why, for God's sake?'

'Payback.' There was something ominous in the way it was said.

'Payback! Payback for what? I've never done anything to you.' He was totally baffled now.

Guppy ignored him. 'And this is just the start; there's plenty more to come.' Seeing Meacher's bewilderment, he asked. 'You really have no idea what I'm talking about? Something in your past perhaps?'

An uneasy look came into John Meacher's eyes at that. In a split second, his demeanour changed from confused anger to one of guarded suspicion. Standing there in the middle of the room, he stared silently at his assistant, waiting to hear what came next.

Guppy saw it and nodded. 'Good, we're getting somewhere. Okay, let's stop fucking about. You call yourself John Meacher but that's not your real name is it?'

Saying nothing, Meacher just watched him, his eyes narrowed slightly.

'No, your real name is David Collins. You began your miserable life in Folkestone on the south coast where your family were fishermen. Good honest work but it wasn't for you, was it? You wanted something better. So you came to London and ended up a petty thief, conman and drug dealer. Then you met a guy called Sam Clark who helped you out when you were attacked by an addict. Do you remember that?' Tom Guppy's voice was withering.

Meacher blinked in surprise. He said nothing though.

'You talked Sam Clark into joining you in a people-smuggling venture bringing immigrants into the country from France. Despite the fact he had a partner and young son to look after, you betrayed him to the authorities and let him take the rap. You never had any intention of sharing the profits with him. I believe you made in the region of £250,000 from that first trip. Do you know what happened to him? That decent man who only wanted to make enough money to look after his family!' There was cold fury in Guppy's voice now. 'They sentenced Sam Clark to twelve years in jail. Six years later, just before he was due to be released early for good behaviour, he was attacked by some nutter who should have been in an asylum and died from head injuries.'

The look on John Meacher's face now was a blend of curiosity and apprehension. He was clearly wondering what the hell was coming next.

'You and your brother Ron did four more runs across

the channel making over a million pounds in the process. It all went wrong on the last run though, didn't it? You got greedy and loaded too many immigrants on the boat. Then, when you hit bad weather and the boat started to capsize, you escaped on the dinghy leaving the poor bastards to drown. After that you decided to go legit. You bought a new name and identity – easy enough to do if you've got the money – and went into the property game. Using the cash you made from the smuggling, you bought up derelict buildings, converted them into flats and rented them out. I know for a fact that you currently own eighty-three properties with a market value of about £11.5 million.

'Eighty-four actually. Your valuation is about right though.'

Guppy paused to light a cigarette before continuing, 'And then you got ambitious and decided to go into politics. You used your wealth to effectively buy the seat in Ely, which of course is not uncommon. Much as I detest you, I have to admit you've been a very good MP and would probably have been an excellent Prime Minister. Except your past has caught up with you so that's not going to happen now, is it?'

Meacher eyed Guppy calculatingly for a few moments before replying, 'Well, you've clearly done your homework. Yes, I admit it – everything you've said is true. So, what now? Blackmail? Money in return for not going to the police.'

Lunging forward suddenly, he thrust his face aggressively into Guppy's. 'Well you can fuck off. Until you can produce hard evidence, it's just allegations. The police will listen politely and then tell you to go away and stop wasting their time.' He stepped back. 'I'm the Prime Minister for God's sake. Do you really think they would take you seriously?'

Not bothering to reply, Guppy just gazed back at him. There was something disconcerting in that flat stare. It gave nothing away.

'How did you find out about me anyway? I thought I'd covered my tracks pretty well.'

'Your accomplice in the people-smuggling operation. Your brother Ron.'

'Never. Ron wouldn't grass on me in a million years. I don't believe you.' He didn't sound too certain though.

Guppy laughed derisively. 'He didn't have much choice really. It was that or have his head blown off. Being a sensible man, he chose to talk.'

For a moment, Meacher seemed to be struggling to credit what he was hearing. Then he shrugged. 'Well, if that's true, I don't suppose I can blame him.' He fixed Guppy with a defiant stare. 'So what though? It doesn't prove a thing. My word against his.'

Picking up a large envelope from a table, Guppy opened it and took out a document. 'This does though. It's an affidavit signed by your brother and it blows the lid on the people-smuggling operation the pair of you carried out. Every detail is there: names, dates, places, figures and more. It'll put you in jail where you belong, you bastard. Eleven immigrants drowned that night when you abandoned them. That's manslaughter, for which the maximum sentence is currently fourteen years. Plus, of course, they'll do you for people-smuggling.'

Meacher snapped, 'Let me see that.' Snatching the document out of Guppy's hand angrily, he sank down into a chair and read it carefully. When he looked up, it was clear the fight was going out of him – he suddenly looked tired, defeated.

Handing the affidavit back, he muttered, 'I seem to be out of options. How much do you want to keep quiet about this?'

'I'm not for sale, you piece of shit,' Guppy said contemptuously.

Meacher stared perplexedly at him. 'Well, what the fuck *do* you want then? What's this all about?'

'I've already told you – it's payback. I'm going to make you pay dearly for what you did to Sam Clark, not to mention those helpless immigrants. Your brother was interviewed at West End Central Police Station this afternoon, arrested and charged. That's one of the things I've been doing the last few days by the way – I went down to Kent to get him. In return for spilling the beans on you, the judge will go easy on him. I have it on good authority that you'll be arrested and charged with manslaughter within the next twenty-four hours.'

He shook his head almost pityingly. 'Not only will you be banged up in a prison cell, you'll be headlining in every newspaper, TV and radio station across the globe. John Meacher, or should I say David Collins, the only British Prime Minister ever to be arrested, never mind put in jail. And all in his first week in the job! You can just imagine what the media will make of that.'

Meacher was having trouble getting his head round it all. 'How on earth did you find out about Ron?' he asked in a puzzled voice. 'And where to find him?'

'Sam Clark told me just before he died in hospital.'

'But you would only have been a young boy.'

'Yes, I was. Nine years old to be precise.'

'Okay, so he told you. But why? What's your connection with him?' Meacher couldn't hide his bafflement.

'He was my father.' Tom Guppy said in a soft voice. 'He wanted me to know the whole story. How you betrayed him and left him to rot in a stinking prison cell.' He glared at Meacher. 'You bastard. My dad lay there on his deathbed and sobbed because he hadn't been able to look after mum and me. I swore I would get even with you one day.' Emotion welling up, he turned away and crossed over to the window where he stood silently looking out.

John Meacher was stunned. He couldn't think of a single word to say. This was a bolt from the blue.

Regaining his composure, Guppy turned back. 'I took my mum's maiden name because they never married and dad was from the wrong side of the tracks. It was easier that way. After he'd gone, she worked night and day to give me a good upbringing and put me through university. A more wonderful, kind, decent woman you couldn't wish to meet. And you ruined her life. She never got over losing him. After I graduated from university, I went down to Kent and had a cosy chat with your brother. He confirmed dad's story and told me you were working as an MP in Ely. As luck would have it, your office was looking for an IT man at the time so I applied for it and got the job. The rest you know.'

Meacher tried one last throw of the dice. 'Tom, it's not too late to stop this. With the right political pressure, the police can be persuaded not to take things further. The same applies to the newspapers. Think about what we've achieved! For the first time in years, this country has a government that's actually getting things done. Employment, investment in infrastructure both up, immigration down, a healthy majority in the Commons. The future is bright. Do you really want to jeopardise all that? For something that happened years ago?'

'You're overestimating your own importance,' Guppy said contemptuously. 'It's you that's fucked, not the government. Your disgrace will be a setback for them but no more than that. It'll be business as usual within a matter of days.'

'I can make you a very rich man Tom. Just name your price.' There was desperation in Meacher's voice now.

Sudden rage contorted Guppy's features. Pulling a bone-handled switchblade from his pocket, he strode across the room to where Meacher stood and raised it to his throat. 'I should do it here and now,' he hissed. 'Like I did with a couple of other bastards who wronged my dad.'

Meacher's eyes bulged in horror at the malevolence in Guppy's eyes. For the first time in his life, he felt real fear as he realised he was literally a split second from death. His knees nearly gave way with relief as his accuser stepped back suddenly and lowered the knife.

Shaking his head, Guppy said, 'But that would be the easy way out for you. Much better that you face a public trial and experience all the disgrace and humiliation that'll go with it. That's why I've invested so much time and effort in helping you get to the top – to make your fall all the more ignominious. Then a long term in prison.'

He raised the blade again, his eyes glittering with menace. 'It's when they eventually let you out that it'll happen. It might be the day after, it might be two years later, but be in no doubt – I will come for you. And when I do …,' Guppy made a slashing motion across Meacher's throat with the knife. 'Every morning when you wake up, you'll be wondering if it's going to be your last day on this earth.'

Grabbing Meacher roughly by the shoulder, he spun him round and marched him to the front door. Opening it, he gave him a friendly pat on the shoulder for the benefit of the security men who he knew would be watching.

'The next time you see me, I'm going to slit your fucking throat. And then my dad will finally have his retribution.'

The End